ESCAPE

Also by Perihan Magden:

Ali and Ramazan
The Messenger Boy Murders
Two Girls

ESCAPE

PERIHAN MAGDEN

TRANSLATED BY KENNETH DAKAN

Text copyright © 2007 by Perihan Magden
English translation copyright © 2012 by Kenneth Dakan

Escape was first published in 2007 by Can Yayinlari as *Biz kimden kaciyorduk Anne?*. Translated from Turkish by Kenneth Dakan. Published in English by AmazonCrossing in 2012.

Quotes from *Bambi* taken from the 1929 Grosset & Dunlap Edition, copyright © 1929, 1931 by Simon and Schuster, Inc.

Published by AmazonCrossing
P.O. Box 400818
Las Vegas, NV 89140

ISBN-13: 9781611091434
ISBN-10: 1611091438
Library of Congress Control Number: 2012940671

To Tülay Tuna:
All books to you, always.

"Most writers, probably, the writers who are most in tune with our time, write about places that have no texture because this is where most of us live."

— ALICE MUNRO

BAMBI

It's been so many years since Mother read it to me.
I haven't forgotten. I'll never forget.
Mother's voice in my ear, reading.
Lines from *Bambi*. Forever.
In Mother's scratchy voice. In that voice of Mother's,
that voice like no other.

NOTHING ABOUT MOTHER is like anyone else. Then again, I can't say I've known anyone else.

"They're all pictures moving before our eyes. As they flow on by, we don't need to remember anything about them. And we won't," Mother says.

We'll just remember what we went through together, Mother. All the good things. The nights you read *Bambi* to me.

In the double bed of a hotel room, propped up against the pillows, the covers pulled up. The two of us are illuminated by the bedside lamp, you reading *Bambi* to me. And *Bambi* isn't just any book. It's important to us.

"It's full of signs," Mother says of *Bambi*. "Rocket flares."

There are two important people in *Bambi*. Two creatures, that is: Bambi and his mother.

Mother's so annoyed at Bambi's mother. I mean, if we met her, came across her in one of the hotels, Mother might beat her up. Teach her a good lesson. That's how mad she is at Bambi's mother.

"If Bambi's mother hadn't been such a fool, hadn't been so careless, Bambi would never have been left alone in the forest. If you're Bambi's mother, you have to stay alive. You must never leave Bambi alone."

I know what Mother means.

Mother would never be foolish or careless, would never leave me motherless. Never.

Alone in the forest.

Mother read that book to me for hours every night. She read and read until I learned to read it myself.

"There's not a children's book in the world I haven't read to you, in English and in Turkish."

But *Bambi*'s different. It's our Book of Prayer. Sometimes we open a page at random and consult a few lines to know whether or not the time has come. Time to move on from the Old Place.

The dangers in *Bambi* are just like our own. Each of them a sign.

My head on Mother's shoulder, or in her lap if I'm very sleepy, I never forget the opening lines of *Bambi*. I'm listening to Mother, filled with anticipation. She's reading in her creaky, croaky voice. She stops from time to time to take a sip of water. Sometimes she pops a cough drop into her mouth.

Mother's been smoking since childhood. Her throat and lungs are worn out. That's what she says.

"What else could I do? I started smoking young. I clung to cigarettes. For comfort, for distraction."

What made Mother so desperate? What happened to her? What happened to her mother? My grandmother?

Mother is reading; her voice in my ear, even now.

He came into the world in the middle of the thicket, in one of those little, hidden forest glades which seem to be entirely open but are really screened in on all sides. There was very little room in it, scarcely enough for him and his mother.

He stood there, swaying unsteadily on his thin legs and staring vaguely in front of him with clouded eyes which saw nothing. He hung his head, trembled a great deal, and was still completely stunned.

"What a beautiful child," cried the magpie.

It's always at this point that Mother stops, looks me directly in the eye, and says, "That's just what the doctors and nurses cried when they saw you."

She says it every time.

So tell me, Mother, were we alone in the hospital? Was no one there with us? Were we always alone? From the beginning?

But I won't ask.

Mother can't bear questions like that.

"Please, baby, don't push me. Please."

I may have done that sort of thing when I was little. Brought up questions that should never be asked. I didn't understand Mother well enough, not yet.

There are questions like that. Questions that must never be asked. Subjects that must never be brought up.

One day, we saw a picture in the newspaper of a baby fox abandoned by its mother.

It gazed, its wide eyes tiny but open. As though seeking help. It had no other choice.

Mother obsessed over that photograph for days. She cut it out and stuck it in the corner of the mirror.

"Abandoned by its mother. Humans are looking after it now. It's getting used to people. Dreadful!"

Actually, we don't usually get newspapers. For this very reason, as well as another: Mother doesn't want news of anyone she knows. She must have been well known. Or her family. Why else would she be so terrified of seeing them in the paper?

But Mother has taught me not to ask unnecessary questions.

Actually, she loves it when I ask questions. As long as they're not the ones that make her fall apart.

When Mother falls apart, she grows weak. Too weak to protect us. She's no longer able to teach them all a lesson.

They're able to hunt us.

"I'm sure they're still after us like a pack of bloodhounds," Mother says.

Just when it seems we're free of them, that they've forgotten all about us: "They'll never forget. That's why I'm not allowed to forget."

We can't depend on them to forget. Just as there's nothing else about them we can depend on.

In order not to be hunted down and caught, we have to be alert, watchful, and suspicious.

When she falls apart—no matter how careful I am, Mother can fall apart for what seems like no reason at all, collapsing in on herself right before my eyes—

When Mother collapses completely, we have to hide, not attracting any attention.

At Those Moments, Mother is in no condition to protect us.

I don't need to do anything.

On the contrary, I must do nothing, see nothing, hear nothing.

"I won't let them defile you," says Mother.

She's so against me being like her. I don't understand why.

Why shouldn't I be like her? She's beautiful, Mother. Perfect in every way.

But I don't have the right to be like her.

"It's because of my past that this is happening."

Mother has a terrible past she never talks about. It's extremely terrible.

Her past is not mine, though.

My past is sparkling clean. And so is my future.

That's what Mother says. The one and only thing in my past is her.

And in my future too.

That's why I'm so happy.

Mother will never be hunted down like Bambi's mother. And I'll never be alone.

I'm not Bambi, even if Mother sometimes calls me "my Bambi."

Mother and me, forever in the forest. Wonderful!

HOTEL TIME

TIME PASSES QUICKLY in hotels.

"Time passes quickly in hotels. Much quicker than in other places," says Mother.

Sometimes the opposite is true. It seems like time has stopped in the hotel.

That's when our spirits sink. When time in the hotel stops. That's when we know it's time to escape.

From our hotel. The New Place has become the Old Place.

It was new when we arrived: the New Place.

Even if we'd been there before.

We do this sometimes. We return to a place we've visited before for a short stay or a long one, a place we used up.

But it's like arriving for the first time.

"We've never been here before. We're here for the first time. Each arrival is a first arrival. It's our first time," says Mother.

Until we use it up and go.

"It's like we've eaten it up and finished it off," Mother says. "We've eaten this place up."

That's when we leave. No matter what time it is.

We can wait at the bus station, the train station, the dock, or the airport; wait until morning for whatever it is that will come and take us away as quickly as possible from the places we've "eaten up" and "finished off."

Mother has an Internal Clock for when we have to leave a hotel, have to spring up and go.

Without checking timetables, tickets, schedules.

It's at times like these that Mother says, "The clock is ticking." Just like the ticking of a time bomb. It can explode and fragment, each bit scattering in a different direction.

Because that's how Mother feels and that's what she says, I feel the same way. The same as her.

Mother and I are alone. There's no one with us.

There never has been and never will be.

Mother hates that word and doesn't want me using it.

"We're not alone," she says. "Never give in to that ugly word. You and I are a unit."

Actually, that's not quite what Mother says.

She says, in English, "We're a unit. We're a Moon Unit."

She says we're a Moon Unit.

It's funny.

It's not funny when Mother says it in English. Mother speaks English sometimes. English gets mixed in with her Turkish.

She gets exasperated, and then she has to teach a lesson to the Girl at Reception, the Busboy, the Pool Attendant, the Hotel Manager, the Travel Agent.

Because we spend our life in hotels, we have to fight with Hotel People and Travel People. To teach them a lesson.

We have no choice. They do ugly things.

Such very ugly things. Really.

Those are the times when Mother has to defend us.

"I have to," Mother says. "I wish they hadn't forced me to teach them a lesson. "Close your ears and eyes real tight, baby, like I taught you. It's time for me to go on the defensive."

I can close my eyes and ears even if they're open. Because that's what mother wants and that's what I must do.

I've learned.

Then, when Mother has gone into Defensive Flight—while she's doing it, I mean, and even if my buttons aren't pushed yet—I hear her mixing English words into her Turkish as she launches the verbal assault.

That's when the Other Side becomes even more confused. Because Mother's words get so confusing. Harder and harder to understand.

"I need to use the possibilities of both languages when I'm on the attack," Mother says.

But I still don't like her mixing so many English words into her Turkish. She should speak only Turkish here.

Lately, we've been staying in Turkey all the time. And we are Turkish, after all. Here, instead of saying "them" and "the others," Mother always says "the Turks."

"The Turks are like that," she says, narrowing her eyes.

"And us, Mother?" I respond, since she and I are Turks, aren't we?

Mother doesn't want to answer. She expects me to understand. And understand I do.

We're a unit: the Moon Unit is what she's named us.

Mother gives special names to the Others too. "The Turks," she'll call them. "Horrid Hordes. Fake Souls. The Bourgeoisie."

Time passes quickly in hotels.

From the beginning, Mother has always wanted me to believe this: that time passes quickly in hotels.

That life in hotels is what's best, what's wonderful, what's right.

"Most important," she often says, "it's what's right. By living in hotels together, we're doing what's right."

Sometimes, time flows incredibly slowly.

Time becomes sticky.

It sticks to our souls, sinking its claws in.

I understand Mother. She feels so terrible at Those Moments. She has trouble breathing.

She doesn't speak. For hours. For days.

Her face darkens with sorrow. Or blanches yellow. Her face turns yellow and black.

"My nerves have made me dark," says Mother. "From sorrow, from worry. Of course, it'll pass. Don't worry, Bambi."

She's scarcely able to get the words out. She expects me to understand.

And I do understand.

I've got no one in life but Mother. If I don't understand *her*, how can I understand anything?

And what can I do?

All I do is read, write, understand Mother. It's also important for me to be a perfect swimmer.

But even when time in the hotel is heavy and sticky, Mother still wants us to stay there sometimes.

Wherever we are.

Whatever hotel we're staying in.

She has to master her Internal Clock. If she doesn't, her Internal Clock will master her.

"It's a form of discipline."

If Mother doesn't get her Internal Clock under control—and hers is a difficult one—it could destroy her. It could destroy us.

Mother's terrified of being destroyed. That's what she fears: her destruction.

And if Mother is destroyed, who will look after me?

Who will protect and defend me? Who will organize our escapes? We're always escaping, the Moon Unit.

Looking after and protecting each other.

If I always look after Mother and protect her, if I always understand Mother, we can survive.

"Then no one can touch us. No one can catch us."

That's what Mother says.

On the outside, our life seems strange. But it isn't.

Because we're on the inside.

And anyway, we have no choice. And we're the only ones who know we have no choice.

That may be true, but it's not such a bad thing.

We're fine.

ALWAYS THE SAME DREAM

SOMETIMES MOTHER WAKES up with a Heavy Heart.

When she's had a bad dream.

Heavy-Heart Days can happen without a dream too.

"I'm sorry, baby," she keeps saying. "I won't be starting the day today."

At times like this, Mother doesn't start the day, can't carry on with it; she wishes only for the day to be done.

The curtains are drawn.

She expects me to have breakfast, swim, and walk on my own. No matter what needs doing that day, I'm to do it on my own, then come back to the room.

Mother doesn't eat on these days. She scarcely drinks water. She says there are thorns in her throat, a lump of asphalt inside her chest.

"Let's not talk, baby. Let's ride the day out in silence, until it's over. Tomorrow, I promise tomorrow will be different. I'll be fine tomorrow. I'll get through the entire day, with you, start to finish. My heart won't drag me down. It won't drag me down to the bottom."

She doesn't have to tell me any of this.

They're words for Heavy-Heart Days. They've collected, piled up. I know them all by heart.

She struggles to get the words out. They stick in her throat. Her eyes fill with tears.

But her eyes are empty.

Like black beads, glassy and wet. Like the eyes of the toys she gets me.

She looks at me with those doll eyes. Eyes that keep apologizing, eyes that keep saying sorry for being so helpless.

Please don't apologize, Mother. Please.

There's this dream. There are a few dreams, actually, but this one in particular.

Mother's in a place like London. A big city. It could be New York. She doesn't know where it is, but it's not Turkey. In the dream, she's in a cafeteria of some kind. She can see the sign. It has a nice name, an unusual name. She never remembers what it is.

But she always remembers that the name was nice and unusual.

"It's a corridor or a hallway," Mother says. "Long and narrow. Full of square little tables with Formica tops."

I know Mother loves Formica tables; she's attached to them.

Once we bought a reddish-orange Formica table at a secondhand store and brought it to our hotel room. We put it out on the balcony and covered it with pebbles. I wished that table were ours. That we could have kept it.

"If we had a home—" I say. "If we have a home one day, I mean—we'll have three or four Formica tables. We'll collect them from secondhand stores. One by one."

Mother loves Formica tables. So do I.

But my wish won't come true. It can't.

I know we have to live in hotels forever.

I know we're on the run.

But now and then, a wish slips out.

It's not that Mother acts as though she hasn't heard. But she acts as though I said a tongue twister, some silly nonsense that spoiled the moment, something wrong.

Mother hates tongue twisters, sayings, and jokes.

"Leave them to the Horrid Hordes. The Fake Souls who pretend to feel, but in truth feel nothing."

We have to live in hotels.

"There's nothing like hotel curtains," says Mother. "Even the most carefully chosen house curtains let in some light."

Mother doesn't want light coming in on Heavy-Heart Days. She says it's easier to shake off the day if she doesn't have to face the light. It doesn't hurt so much.

In this dream of Mother's, in this long, narrow cafeteria whose name she never manages to remember, she's standing and talking to someone. She's on her feet, because she's about to say something to someone and go outside.

And that's why everything happens right before her. Right under her nose. Right at her feet.

In the dream a stray dog, long-legged and white, comes inside and collapses on the floor. It's making such a pitiful yelping sound.

"Like a wailing baby. But it's for a short time only. It makes a heart-scorching plea, like it's begging to be let go. Then it stops."

The dog begins writhing on the floor. Those are its last cries. The last sounds it makes.

When Mother looks down, she's horrified to see that a piece of glass has been used to cut the dog's throat from ear to ear. She sees the piece of glass right there on the floor. Blood is gushing from the dog's cut throat.

"Please! It's dying! The dog's dying! Quick! Quick!" Mother starts screaming. She's choking on her own helplessness and horror.

It's a dream scream: impossible to hear.

The others are in a panic. They don't know what to do either. The dog is on the floor fighting for its life. But Mother has taken all the horror everyone else feels and made it her own. It's hers, and it is for the others in the dream that she can't breathe. She's gasping. Again and again.

"What kind of person would cut a stray dog's throat with a piece of glass? How could anyone be so horrible?"

It's just a dream, Mother. The nightmare that's been bothering you for years. Come on, let's stitch up the dog's throat. Let's have him get up on his feet. Think of it like that. Let's please imagine it that way. Please.

Mother can't stand the sight of dogs, especially white ones.

She says the dogs in her dreams make her so sad that she doesn't want to see another one, ever again. Especially a white one.

"And anyway," she says, on a good day, when her heart is light and right in its place, "what else could a white dog mean; its throat cut with a piece of glass, fighting for its life? It's not like I don't know."

There's nothing Mother doesn't know.

She doesn't know how to get up on a bad day, that's all.

"That's why you should never feel bad. I'm used to it, used to myself. But I couldn't bear to see you feeling bad. Couldn't bear to see you being dragged down by a heavy heart."

I'll never feel bad, Mother.

There's no reason for me to feel bad.

You always take measures. You don't even allow me to get a cold.

"If I have to, I'll lick you, lick away all the sickness, from your body and soul. Shaman-mother!"

My mom the shaman. My beautiful mother. Dear Mommy.

I'm terrified of upsetting Mother, though.

More than anything.

I live with the fear every day.

I can't get a cold, even. I mustn't.

"You haven't come down with a single childhood illness."

Mother says this as though I've been given supernatural powers.

It's because of the fear that I don't get sick, Mother.

I'm afraid of worrying you.

One day that fear will cause my heart to stop.

That's what I'm afraid of.

Other than that, my heart's like a bird. It never gets heavy.

It'll never get heavy.

My love for you is wings for my heart.

Don't worry. Nothing bad will ever happen to me to upset you.

Never.

THE GIRL AT RECEPTION

OF COURSE I noticed them.

Who wouldn't?

A mother and daughter. And they stayed for such a long time.

But after a while, near the end, they'd been here for so long, we stopped noticing them so much.

We'd gotten used to them.

And then, when it happened, and they left so suddenly, I mean, when they ran away, we all said, "Something like this was bound to happen."

People do that after the fact. You know, when something so completely unexpected happens. We act as though we expected it all along.

Well, for starters, they were just such an unlikely pair. As if they didn't belong together. Mismatched. Somehow they seemed wrong for each other.

How else can I put it? Anyway, that's what we thought when we first saw them.

It's true, no one expects daughters to be miniature versions of their mothers. Mothers and daughters don't have to look one bit alike.

But the two of them, this mother and daughter, well, I think it was the pool boy who put it best. Or it may not have been him, I can't remember for sure who said it. But I remember us talking about them when they first arrived.

"You mean that woman *produced* that girl?" someone said.

The guy who looks after the pool, yeah, it was him. He said it.

The word *produced* somehow stuck.

Then we must have gotten used to them. We stopped talking about them so much. We only mentioned them when we saw something extra weird.

Not that they ever did anything weird. It was that they were so weird themselves.

Now how do I put this? It's like they were trying too hard to fit in. They were trying too hard.

Especially the mother. Especially her.

It's like she was hiding something. Like she was hiding from everyone and everything.

And as for the girl, there was no way for her to blend in. She attracted too much attention.

Let me tell you, she was the most beautiful girl I've ever seen in my entire life.

The most beautiful girl I've ever seen, even in the movies.

There was no way not to look at that girl, not when she was out and about, I mean: heading for the pool, on the way back to her room, on the way to breakfast, when they came down to eat, when they came back from a walk, passing by, right in front of me—

The reception desk faces the main entrance, as in all hotels, so it's us who see the guests the most.

Even if we don't want to.

Sometimes I feel like I've seen too many people, more than my fair share of arrivals and departures, of entrances and exits.

I don't want to see any more people, I say to myself sometimes.

But that's one luxury I'll never have. You're always seeing, always registering. Who comes in and who goes out, who changes into a fresh outfit, who gets drunk, who still hasn't gotten over a call put through to their room, who was late for breakfast and on the verge of tears as they ordered a continental breakfast, who takes it out on you because their shirt isn't back from the cleaners, or finds something else to take out on you.

I mean, ugh.

And no matter how hard you try not to, you keep registering and recording. With friends, I call it the "receptionist's black box."

So, as I said, there was no way not to notice that girl. She was the most beautiful, well-behaved, glowing kid in the world. It wasn't normal. She was too beautiful. Too much.

It might have been different if that woman hadn't been her mother—that dried-up old bat, all shriveled up from bad nerves.

Actually, it's more like she was ageless.

You couldn't have guessed her age.

Because every now and then—but only rarely—you'd see she'd done her hair up in a ponytail; we'd see her wearing something new, smiling a little, wishing you good morning, asking how you were, thanking you, and things like that. Normal things.

Keep in mind that they stayed for a few months and I'm talking about only four or five occasions. But now, when I come to think of it, I can say that every once in a while she seemed all right. I mean, the mother wasn't always sick.

And at times like that, when she was well, she looked ten or fifteen years younger. Like the girl's big sister or something. Like a big sister, dark and kind of pretty, but completely different from the girl.

She was so thin. Exactly what they mean by "skin and bones." One day she wore a striped shirt over a pair of jeans. I remember it clearly: navy blue and white stripes, a long shirt, untucked. She'd gathered her hair up above her neck. They came in from outside. From a walk. Her hair had come loose, bits of it were falling around her long, thin face.

I can't tell you how good she looked that day.

Like she'd turned into someone else, another woman. That's the kind of mother a beautiful girl should have, I remember thinking to myself. But most of the time you couldn't help thinking they didn't go together.

It bothered you.

Those hands, thin and ropy; that face, cut off and distant, like she was looking through you or past you but never at you. When you talked to her, you'd look at her hands, not her face. It seemed as if that's what she wanted you to do, as if you had no choice. She had that kind of power over people.

"I wonder if that woman kidnapped that beautiful girl?" Those were the words that popped out of my mouth one day as they walked off. I'll never forget it. It was such a horrible thing to say.

But she got on your nerves with that sour face and the way she looked right through you. There was something about her that made people say and do the wrong thing.

Later, we joked about it a lot: "Did she steal that gorgeous kid?"

When that girl walked by, you couldn't take your eyes off her.

What's she wearing? How'll she greet us? What's her hair like today? Is she wearing one of those weird hats? What will she say when she drops off the key, picks up the key, walks past the desk?

You know how people never seem to get enough of famous types, those celebrities on TV? How everything they do seems so special?

But she was just a girl. Just a girl staying in the hotel, with her shriveled-up mother. Why get so worked up about her?

She was probably about thirteen or fourteen. She could have been fifteen, but looked younger. She was always dressed in kid colors. Weird stuff. Like her clothes were picked out to make her look younger.

Kids don't dress like that anymore. They don't talk like that either. I'm not sure they ever did.

She was different. From another world. Straight out of the movies. From some strange place you know nothing about and aren't used to.

She sure was pretty, though. Such a beauty. Those long lashes, huge eyes, tiny nose. And she was so well mannered and charming. You just melted at the sight of her.

We had this contest, who'd spot her most. Like the more times you saw her, the better the day would be.

"I saw her six times. A whole six times!" That's how we competed. It was a stupid game.

I'm sure that the mother's complete loneliness and weirdness only made us even more obsessed with the girl.

And we sure were—obsessed, I mean. "Have you seen her yet today?" "I haven't seen her anywhere. She hasn't even been down at the pool. It's been such a shitty day; the manager's being such a jerk, sticking it to us every way he can."

We turned her into some kind of good-luck charm.

How can I put it?

We used her.

As though she weren't real; as though she were a fantasy, a dream, an angel.

Seeing her did us good. But what about her? How was she?

When I think about what happened, I feel so ashamed of myself.

We could have helped. We could have tried to rescue her.

But I don't know; could we have? Could we have rescued her?

We didn't understand a thing, not a thing.

It just never occurred to us.

I guess people don't see what they don't want to. Not with their eyes, and not with their hearts.

PEBBLES

WE'RE USUALLY AT the seaside.

We stay in rooms with a sea view. Close enough to walk to the sea.

Deserted little seaside towns. Undiscovered or fallen out of fashion. Never in seasons the Horrid Hordes prefer. If they come, we go.

Mother's afraid of crowded places. Of fashionable places.

"No one, absolutely no one in the entire world, is as nauseating as a member of the Turkish upper class."

We don't belong to a class; that's what Mother says. We have money, but we don't belong to a class.

We always stay at the best hotels. In the biggest rooms with the best views.

But we used to go to even more expensive hotels. We used to go abroad more often.

Now we stay where others don't, in seaside hotels either abandoned or neglected as they wait for visitors.

We walk along the shore. Sometimes we spend the whole day collecting pebbles. And cockleshells, of course.

We go down to the shore with cloth bags. When the bags are full to bursting, we go back to our room.

Sometimes we go down to the shore three or four times in a single day. Mother can't get enough of collecting the pebbles.

"Pebbles prove that at least some things are perfect. They've got a language of their own; each of them is beautiful in its own way. We understand them. Each of them is telling us something, and we understand."

We wash them one by one in the basin in the bathroom. Sometimes it gets clogged with sand. We have to lie when we telephone reception to get it fixed.

"We can't tell them the drain got clogged from the sand we washed off our pebbles and shells," Mother says. "You'll find something to tell them, won't you, Bambi?"

We line the pebbles up, all in a row. When they haven't lost their other halves, the cockleshells look like butterflies. On the coffee tables, the nightstands, the tables.

If we've been somewhere for a long time, even the spare bed overflows with them.

"Pick two or three," Mother says, later. "We can't fit more than that in your bag."

When I was little, I'd cry as I picked three out; I'd cry and beg Mother to let me take more.

That's the beauty of pebbles, Mother says: they don't form any attachments.

"They rest on the seashore. Pebbles and cockleshells more beautiful than you could ever imagine, resting on seashores across the world, waiting. For you. Hoping you'll come and find them. Hoping against hope."

I choose three pebbles. Mother sometimes chooses one.

We take the rest of them back in our bags. On the last day. The last night. To the beach, where they belong.

But sometimes, the going-all-of-a-sudden times, we leave them in the room.

It makes me want to cry. It's as if we've taken them from their mothers, their friends, their homes; now we're leaving them all in the room and running off.

"Pebbles don't have mothers, Bambi," Mother says. "Don't worry; I'm leaving a note."

Mother writes a note to the hotel people. She asks them to return the pebbles to the beach, and encloses some money.

"They do it if you enclose money; don't worry."

It's the same with our clothing.

Nearly all our clothing, and our shoes, our hats, our flip-flops, our books, toys, pillows, lamps. Everything we got while we stayed there, we leave behind.

No more than a small knapsack, and no check-in baggage whatsoever.

Travelers without baggage: that's us.

"If we're weighed down, they'll catch us, baby. We've got to travel light, always travel light. We can get the same things anywhere."

Mother always wears the same things. Shirts and T-shirts in black or white, hooded jackets, blue jeans, boots with thick soles.

When something gets old, she gets another. And when she can't find the exact same thing, she gets upset and angry.

But she shops for me all the time. Things in pale pink, baby blue, bright green, and light yellow. The right colors for fair-haired, fair-skinned little girls, Mother says. She says they look good on me.

"But they're baby colors! I want to wear black too. Hooded jackets, loose jeans, dark shirts. Like you, Mother."

"Baby, are you unhappy? Is that what you're trying to tell me?"

I wouldn't mind dressing like a child. But she dresses me like a baby. Like a doll. It's getting so difficult to find my clothes in the colors she chooses. I've grown up.

"What about you, Mom? Are you unhappy? Are you always unhappy?"

Mother never denies it.

"After so much sorrow, I expect I'll never know happiness."

Mother says she could die of unhappiness. She could have died and she almost did. Then she found out she was pregnant with me. She found out just in time. When she was about to die.

"I stayed alive for you. The joy you brought kept me alive."

But the joy I brought and the peace we get from our way of life aren't enough to lighten Mother's unhappiness.

When those waves of sorrow crash over her, when they turn our life upside down, it's during Those Moments that I want more than ever to learn about Mother's past. Our Past.

Who's my father? Is it from him that we're running all the time? Did my father not want me to be born? Does he not want us to be alive? Or did everything happen because of my mother's mother and her father? Are they after us? What do they want from us? What can they do to us? Do they want to kill us? If so, why? Who are we running from, Mother?

Mother won't let me ask any of these questions.

When I do, she gets so sad and sick that I can't bring myself to ask anything anymore.

She says she'll tell me everything one day.

"I'll tell you everything one day; please be patient, baby. You'll grow up. I'll get better. Then I'll tell you everything. You'll understand. You'll see I was right. There's a reason for everything we do. We've got to keep running. They're following us."

You're right, Mother. I mustn't push you into Those Moments. What if you can't come back again? What if something happens to you? What if you're never able to return to normal life, our life?

Everything we collect, buy, pick out, so carefully, is left in hotel rooms. We shut the door behind us and go.

If Mother finds she can't bear the pattern of the hotel curtains or the synthetic touch of the bedspread, if there's anything she just can't bear—

We go and get ourselves our own bedspreads. We pin our new curtains over the hotel ones. We get ourselves towels, gray, purple, and maroon. We drape our own fabrics over the armchairs.

Then we have to leave everything and run.

Escape to a new place. To a new hotel.

"Don't get upset over anything, Bambi," says Mother. "Don't get attached to anything. It's enough that we're attached to each other. We don't need anything else."

I don't get attached to anything, Mother.

Once I got a little attached to Fetus, but that's it.

My attachment to you is enough.

Your attachment to me is enough for me.

I know how we have to live. We can't be weighed down, so it's easy to escape. So they don't catch us.

Staying alive is essential.

So you don't die of unhappiness.

Since you stayed in this world for me, I've got to be here for you. Just like you said, like you want me to.

"We've got no choice."

I know.

A SMALL TABLE

"WE DON'T CARE what they say or what they think. Try not to talk to them or hear a word they say. Or we'll find ourselves involved in banalities. We'll find ourselves lost in the middle of their world."

It's very important to Mother.

I mustn't listen to others.

I mustn't hear what others say.

We have a world all our own. We're the Moon Unit.

"We're the Moon Unit," says Mother. "Be sure not to let them dump their filth into our world."

They always talk about such boring things.

About such vulgar things.

Things that don't interest us, things that mustn't interest us.

They have cell phones they're forever shouting into, as if their phones make them invisible, inaudible.

They talk about their families.

They talk about their boyfriends and girlfriends.

But most of all they talk about money.

No matter how often Mother warns me, sometimes I can't resist. I hear them. I listen.

We have less and less money.

Mother had a lot of money when I was born. I know that.

But because we've been on the run ever since I was born, because we've had to live in hotels—

We don't go to faraway countries as often now.

We don't change countries nearly as often now.

When we run out of money, Mother goes and withdraws more from the bank.

But I have a feeling we have less and less money.

Still, we mustn't talk about money. We mustn't give in.

We can never allow them to get in our souls and poison us.

But somehow they get to us, poisoning our souls, "contaminating" us, as Mother says.

They categorize. And they're incredibly rude. It drives Mother crazy. It stings and angers her.

"They try to look down on us," Mother says. "It's a form of punishment for being outside their experience. How ugly; how shameful!"

Each room has a table reserved in the hotel dining room.

That's the system in this hotel. A table is assigned for the duration of your stay.

When we come down, we find a metal triangle with our room number resting on a table. We're meant to sit at that table. Our table.

"So we're meant to sit at this table?" says Mother, her eyebrows arched high into the air.

It's a small table, perhaps big enough for one, two, let's say. It's tiny.

Mother looks around the room.

I follow her eyes. I know what she's looking for; I know what she's looking at.

Nowhere, in the entire dining hall, is there a single table as small as the one that has been assigned to us. Even worse, our table is jammed between two huge ones.

Our table is positioned so that if people get up from the two huge tables on either side, we have to stand up to allow them to pass. We have to stand up, again and again.

It's the smallest table. It's the most cramped, the most uncomfortable table. We have to stand up repeatedly, every time they get up to fill their plates. At the open buffet.

When we've finished our meal, Mother summons the Headwaiter. "Let's see what Pumpkin Face has to say about this."

Pumpkin Face makes his way over to our table.

With great difficulty. Dragging his feet.

Mother points: husbands and wives, pairs of lovers, couples, all of them consisting of a man and a woman.

They're all sitting at tables for four. Tables that aren't jammed between two others, normal-sized tables in nice locations.

Mother points to the tables one by one.

Pumpkin Face pretends not to understand. "Yes, madam?" he says to Mother. "And how may I be of assistance?"

"You may not," says Mother. "I'm not requesting assistance. Are you aware that not a single table in the entire dining hall is as small as the one at which we're seated?"

As the Headwaiter repositions the water jug on the table, he assumes expressions: of bewilderment, distress, of a busy man in a great hurry. The moment he hits on the magic word, he'll bolt. He takes several deep breaths. Mother might acknowledge his distress and set him free. Or so he hopes.

"That there's even room on this table for a water jug, along with two plates, is something of a miracle, is it not? Actually, this table could be more accurately described as an end table. An end table jammed between two enormous tables."

"What do you mean?" Headwaiter asks. He's realized that nothing will save him from Mother. He tries to conceal his growing annoyance.

"What I mean," says Mother, "is this: Due to the simple fact that we happen to be a mother and daughter, we have been assigned a table—an end table, to be more precise—an end table considered unworthy of any of the other couples, the *sacred* couples, in this room. You feign ignorance. You pretend not to have noticed the appalling conditions under which two of your guests have endured their dinner. That is precisely what you are doing at this very moment."

"There wasn't another table," says Headwaiter. He's begun to panic. Mother's creaky, croaky voice is that amazing.

"You decided that this table was appropriate for us," says Mother. "A table at which a man and a woman would never be seated; we're two females: a mother and daughter, a strange, most unusual circumstance. Naturally, you present *us* with this intolerable table; that's it, isn't it?"

"We'll change it immediately," says Headwaiter. He's breathing hard now. Furious, but fully aware it's best to admit defeat. "Show me where you'd like to sit. I'll have it ready for breakfast."

"Any table will do. Any table but this one," says Mother. "A table for four, like the ones where the sacred couples are sitting. And, it goes without saying, a table that isn't jammed between two others. The kind of table you considered appropriate for everyone else: that is, for the couples comprised of a man and a woman. I also ask that your discourtesy not go unpunished. Not only are you discourteous and thoughtless, you pretended nothing is wrong, instead of simply apologizing immediately and resolving the matter."

"That's going a bit far," Headwaiter chokes.

As Mother stands, her chair tips over. Now everyone is watching. Those who haven't heard her words hear her chair crash.

She takes my hand, and we begin walking.

"You know full well that I haven't gone far at all—not yet—but if I wished to, I could go very far indeed."

We leave the dining hall.

Mother decides that the hotel is poisonous. We go up to our room and gather our things.

We don't have much. We always travel light. Let's leave this horrible place, where they gave us a small table.

Broken and wounded, without letting anything else happen.

Let's escape right away, Mother.

Don't let them drag you down. Let's escape right away, before you teach them a lesson.

THE SNOWSTORM

"Shall we kill a mouse, too, sometime?"
"No," replied his mother.
"Never?" asked Bambi.
"Never," came the answer.
"Why not?" asked Bambi, relieved.
"Because we never kill anything," said his mother,
simply.
Bambi grew happy again.

MOTHER'S SCRATCHY VOICE is enfolding me. Blanketing me.

I'm still little. Still at an age when Mother reads me *Bambi*. My head in her lap. We're the only ones sitting in a row of five seats. On an empty plane. Completely empty.

"Put your legs up, Bambi," Mother says.

I sleep all the way to New York.

We're flying from London to New York. We couldn't fly the night before. We waited at the London airport for hours.

Mother took me to a room far away from the announcements. We read and watched television and waited for hours. Mother wanted me to sleep. But I couldn't.

Every once in a while, she went out into the corridor to look at the screen and said, "Delayed again," every time she came back into the room. "Again. Again."

The restless waiting kept me awake. Mother was oddly happy. The Snowstorm delaying our flight seemed to be making her happy.

"Delayed again," her voice rang out. "Apparently we'll be spending the night in an airport hotel. Compliments of British Airways! Because of the Snowstorm, even if they did manage to take off, they may not be able to land."

Sharing a disaster with others exhilarates Mother, I know that now.

Perhaps we're not alone. Perhaps we're not the only ones weighed down. It happens to them too; it can happen to them too.

Mother was thrilled that we'd be spending the night in an airport hotel in London. I don't know how I've managed to remember so many details. Some of the details of that night are still so clear in my mind, sharp as glass.

Not all of them, though. Not everything. I can't remember some of the things that happened the next day at that hotel in Union Square once we finally got to New York, can't remember them at all.

But I do remember Union Square: the hotel. I remember where we tried to stay, in Union Square.

"Union Square," Mother says as we get into the taxi. I hear her voice in my ear, even now, exactly the way it sounds as she is instructing the driver.

Our plane had finally taken off from London, after many
more delays.

Now we're waiting for a taxi in the middle of the Snowstorm
in the middle of the night.

In front of the airport in New York. In a snowstorm.

It's blinding. "In a fucking blizzard!" Mother says as we wait
outside, in line for a taxi.

One pulls up every ten or fifteen minutes. The line is long;
we're at the end.

"All this baggage," Mother says. We wait in the biting cold.
And wait.

"Baby, are you cold?" Mother keeps asking. She rubs my
mittened hands between her gloved ones. She unties and reties
the earflaps of my cap. She winds my scarf tight.

"Please don't get cold, Bambi. Whatever you do, don't get
ill. Don't get ill on account of my thoughtlessness. Why, oh why,
did we travel with baggage? We could have gotten everything we
needed in New York."

I never get sick, so that mother won't get sad. I'm not shivering as we wait for a taxi that night. I never shiver. Mother, I'm
fine.

I remember Mother saying with the sharpness of glass, "To
Union Square" as we get into the taxi. Mother's voice is square
and sharp.

I remember struggling into that little hotel. Mother is lug-
ging our suitcase up those icy steps.

The hotel, that hot and tiny hotel; now we're inside.

A nightmare; I remember certain details of the inside of that
hotel so clearly. Such a strange mixture, some things remembered so clearly, some not remembered at all. Like the morning
after a nightmare.

The Man at Reception is huge. A giant of a man. Really. He's wearing a baseball cap and a gray sweatshirt. He has a beard. A long red beard. Bloodred.

As he pounds his fist on the desk, an Elvis doll nods and bobs. The man's Elvis doll, guitar rocking, head bobbing. Written in bold green letters on his gray sweatshirt is the word TENNESSEE.

The Man at Reception must be very angry at Mother. As he pounds and pounds, the head bobs, the guitar rocks. He rocks so much I'm terrified he'll fall facedown onto the wooden desktop. My eyes are on Elvis. I pray he doesn't fall.

"What? What do you mean you don't accept credit cards at this time of night?" Mother says. "I haven't got that kind of cash on me at the moment. I'll withdraw some money from the bank first thing in the morning."

"Why not just go get it now? There's an ATM only two blocks away, what are you waiting for?" He makes the rules around here. He doesn't have to let you stay, not at this time of night. Elvis rocks and rocks, crazed.

"Cash!" he shouts. "If I say cash, you pay cash!"

"In this fucking blizzard?" Mother says. "With a child?"

The Giant Man at Reception answers with a bunch of "fucks."

All kinds of "fucks" fly through the air. "Fucking" and "fuck" and "fucked."

"You fucking fascist, racist redneck," I hear Mother say to him. "It's because of our passports, isn't it?"

My eyes are on Elvis when Mother says this. Elvis falls flat on his face on the desktop. Giant Man says one more thing to Mother. One more thing before his voice stops.

As Mother reaches for something on the desktop, she says again, "It's because of our passports, isn't it, redneck?"

Strange, the Giant Man's red beard is getting redder. It's getting darker right before my eyes.

Mother wipes her hands on a wet wipe pulled out of her purse.

"Come on, Bambi, we're getting out of here."

I'm cold now. I'm shivering. I'm freezing, Mother. I always keep from shivering so you won't get sad. I hold it inside and make it go away.

But I'm so cold now.

"Come on, baby!" Mother says. Her voice is terrible. I start to cry.

We're walking on the sidewalk. Mother's tugging our suitcase, struggling.

My cheeks are wet; they sting. The more I wipe them with my mittens, the more they sting.

My nose burns. And my cheeks keep stinging.

Never cry in a blizzard.

Mother tugs the suitcase along with one hand and me with the other, along the icy sidewalk. She stops now and then and kicks the suitcase. "If we leave it here, they'll open it up and go through it, they'll know who we are."

We cross the street. "We've got to get far away from the hotel," Mother says. "Hang on until the next corner, baby."

We cross at the corner. The suitcase, cause of all our troubles, gets another kick from Mother.

"Quick, send us a taxi." Looking up at the sky, those are Mother's words.

"Mom, look, a taxi's coming!" I scream. In the middle of the Snowstorm in the middle of the night, a taxi stops right in front of us.

"Straight to the airport," Mother says. "We've got a plane to catch."

We haven't got a plane; we haven't got a ticket. We wait for hours in the airport.

We're returning to London on the first flight. We'll never set foot in New York City again.

After that city we'll never have baggage again. That might be why I remember the Snowstorm. Or it might be because the cold hurt so much. We'll have to fit everything into a small backpack, which is good and bad. Just like never seeing New York again.

THE POOL BOY

EARLY IN THE morning and late in the day, that's when she'd swim.

Every day. Every damn day.

Doesn't she ever get sick of it, I'd think to myself. Doesn't she ever get tired?

Doesn't it ever get to be too much? And the mother. Always that woman.

They were always the first to arrive in the morning. And the last to go at night.

When they were done, I'd switch off the lights and lock the gates. That's how late it was.

She'd watch and wait for everyone to go.

She said as much. "It's better to swim when no one's around," she said.

The girl was swimming laps. That witch of a mother making her, like a trainer.

But she didn't look like she had any complaints. Always smiling, real sweet. She talked real sweet too, like when she asked for something.

This one time she asked me, "Could you make it a little warmer tomorrow?" It was chilly outside. She must have gotten cold training.

I got so excited I went weak at the knees. The way she looked at me, right in the eye, and that little voice—

And that was after I got used to her. I mean, when I wasn't getting butterflies in my stomach anymore.

Like I did the first time I saw her; I'd never seen a girl like that. She was even prettier than those girls in the TV shows and videos.

But a lot younger than them. Just a child still. She was definitely about five or six years younger than me. That much I'm sure of.

She was slender. And tall. You couldn't really guess her age. She talked in that soft voice, that little-girl voice.

It was funny, it was like the two of them were trying to make her seem younger, trying to keep her real age a secret or something.

The mother was always there, right next to her. Always the mother.

As if she spent all her time and energy keeping her daughter away from everyone else. So no one could get close. So she couldn't become friends with anyone. So people couldn't see her, even out of the corner of their eye.

She was like a hawk, always on the lookout. You could feel it.

And that's why the girl was like a windup doll. Talking in that baby voice and making you feel all funny. And kind of scared.

It was as if she weren't real. Like a girl robot. Too pretty, too polite, too good to be true. Just too much.

You didn't dare get close. Didn't dare try to have a word or two.

That's exactly what that witch of a mother wanted: to have her daughter all to herself.

She wanted to be her whole life. Like a guard, a prison warden, a hostage taker.

That's it in a nutshell: the girl was being kept hostage by that woman. A hostage, the same as in the movies.

They didn't look a bit alike. Not one bit! You'd expect a daughter to look like her mother, at least a little bit. Well, wouldn't you?

So, how do we know for sure if that lady was the girl's mother? You see things like that in the news all the time. Some crazy broad steals a baby, from a hospital or whatever.

That witch could have been a nurse. She could have stolen the girl when she was just a baby. I mean, kidnapped her right after she was born.

Picture a strip of rawhide. A leather strap. A dried-out old branch. That's what she was like. Dark and all dried up.

And boy was she nasty. There I'd be, heart pounding in my mouth, afraid she'd say something.

But she didn't really talk much. Hardly talked at all.

She hardly talked to her daughter. Probably because I was there. I'm sure they talked together a lot, understood each other real well. I could feel it.

Her, holding onto that stopwatch as she watched her daughter finish swimming fifty meters, freestyle; her daughter looking up into her mother's eyes, happy as can be. "Twenty-seven seconds, that's a split second faster," she'd say. "Baby, that's nearly a world record for your age group."

She always called her "baby" or "Bambi." I guess the name came from that movie for kids. You know, the one where they shoot the fawn's mother. The one with the deer. You know.

The mother would stretch out on one of the deck chairs, always a book in her hand. She smoked nonstop, one after another. Sometimes she'd swim. But not very often.

If she didn't smoke so much, she'd have been some swimmer though. You wouldn't believe it, it was something to see!

"My breaststroke was excellent when I was your age. But my freestyle was never as good as yours," she'd say to her daughter.

They always talked about the same things. I listened and listened until I must have memorized every word they said.

Turns out the mother swam too, was a swimmer when she was her daughter's age. It's so hard to picture her like that. Young, I mean.

But there was something about the way she'd hold onto that stopwatch, the two of them celebrating the daughter's time, together, looking at each other, their eyes all shiny—

You were like, that witch really loves that girl. It was really something, the love I mean, so strong and strange, so different—

It was clear as day. You felt it. And when you felt it, you'd feel kind of guilty.

It's none of your business! They're just a mother and daughter. If they want to swim all day, so be it. They're both happy. What it's to you?

But it was creepy too. It was suspect. They were so alone. They stayed for so long. They were so—it's hard to put it into words—so separate.

They happened to be at the pool one day when the hotel manager came round. As usual, the guy was trying to assert himself. Well, did he ever meet his match or what! "Go on over," he says to me, "and tell that woman there's no smoking in the pool area."

Boy did she lay into him!

The others, the fat ladies, aren't like that. They mouth off, but only to me. Well this witch goes straight for the manager!

How can smoking be banned, she says, when ashtrays have been placed everywhere, and on and on. The kind of thing that wouldn't be so hard to take if a normal person said it, in a normal way. You know, the kind of thing you'd just shrug off.

But the way she laid into the manager! Not just what she said. Bad as it was. It was the way she said it. Who'd have thought a string of words could be said with such hate, such venom.

I've never heard anything like it. And I hope I never do again.

That's when I thought to myself, there's something seriously wrong with that lady. I mean, it was clear from the start that they weren't normal, that they were up to no good.

Something wasn't right; and you thought, sooner or later there's going to be trouble. I swear that's exactly what ran through my mind the day she blew up at the manager.

Of course later, after what happened—when I said I'd seen it coming—everyone at the hotel made fun of me. So, Mister Detective, if you've got such a good nose, why didn't you warn anyone? they said. Why didn't you have them thrown out? Why didn't you run over to the military police? Why didn't you do something? they all said. On and on, mocking me for days.

It doesn't dawn on you until it's too late. Not just what happens here at the hotel, but all the time.

You can see the woman's off her head, but then there's the girl. How could you do anything to her? Even if you got wise to the woman, you just can't bring yourself to hurt the girl.

When I look back on it now, I can see that the girl was like a piece of scenery, up on the stage. So you're staring, all stupid-like, at the girl; she's so pretty and sweet you can't take your eyes off her—and all the while the mother's doing what she has to do, messing things up.

But there's more to it than that. If she hadn't had such a pretty daughter, maybe she wouldn't have lost her marbles watching over her all the time. Or if they hadn't been so alone, maybe?

But I felt it, I knew it. Something told me the day she went after the manager. That's when it hit me: if that's what she does with her tongue, who knows what she'll do with her hands. That's what I said to myself.

That woman's capable of anything. That's exactly what I said to myself.

FACES

NO MATTER WHERE we go, Mother finds toys that "deserve to be bought." Toys that are waiting for us. Ones full of "meaning."

No matter where we go.

They're in the most unlikely places. Bus stations, beachside food stands, airport shops, stationery stores, curiosity shops, pharmacies.

"Look carefully, and you'll see that toys are sold everywhere. Shopkeepers can't help it; they always keep a few toys on hand. It's not that they expect to make a sale, it's that they too want some toys in their lives."

If we can't find any, toys that is, we fill our hotel rooms with floats. Inflatable rafts shaped like turtles, tubes with big dog heads, a Mickey Mouse splash pool, armband floats with duck heads, a shark boat.

Pebbles and toys. We can't get enough of them. They turn a hotel room into a home; isn't that so, Mother? Into home?

I love watching Mother with a toy she's just taken off the shelf, turning it over, round and round. Her eyes glow; her mouth softens. Happy, smoothed.

She puts the toy back and gets another, the same one. Then another, and another. She looks and looks at their faces. Because only one of them is there for us. Is there, waiting for us.

"Baby, look closely at the faces of the dolls and animals. Even if they're one of hundreds, thousands made by the Chinese, even if they're horribly mass produced, each has a face different from the others. One's lips are pursed, one's eye has slipped down, one's hair is flatter on one side. To the discerning eye, each of them is one of a kind, unique."

My one and only mommy. You're unique.

In the old days, when we used to stay in big cities, we'd get a lot more toys. Returning to our hotel every day, our arms and hands were always full of packages.

Until it was as if we were living in a toy shop secretly moved into the hotel. And the more we filled our room, the more amazed the hotel cleaners would be.

But just like the pebbles, we had to leave them all behind, suddenly.

When Mother sensed danger, a threat; when she sensed that they'd be able to follow our tracks to the Old Place, we'd abandon them and go.

I got used to leaving everything behind in hotel rooms. We have to travel light, have to grab our bags and go. We had to pick up and go.

We were Passengers without Baggage: we always were. Passengers on the run. Passengers who have to disappear without a trace.

But when I was little—six or seven—we picked out a stuffed Bambi in London. It was huge! As big as me.

Sometimes I'd climb on top of it, a big pillow. I'd wrap my arms around its neck, nice and soft, and fall asleep.

"What do you mean, baby? Take Bambi?"

I wanted to take it with us on a walk. To carry it in my arms.

"Your Bambi's even bigger than *my* Bambi, bigger than you," Mother says. "Let's leave it in the room; it'll be here for you when we return."

"But Bambi's sick of staying inside," I say. "He wants to go on a walk too." I'm still little. I still get things into my head. I still expect to get my own way.

"Baby, stop acting so spoiled," Mother says. "Please, stop wearing me out. Look, your mommy's worn out."

Mother's always worn out. I mustn't wear her out even more. Or we won't be able to run away. She won't be able to help me escape. They'll catch us.

We're leaving behind our London hotel room, all full of toys. Overflowing with toys.

"You can pick one, baby," Mother says.

I pick Bambi. My brother.

"It's such a big toy," Mother says. "Don't pick that one, why don't you pick one you can carry?"

"Uh-uh," I say. "Uh-uh. Uh-uh." Again and again, over and over.

"Let's take this one; this one's so cute," Mother says. "It's Bashful, one of the seven dwarves. Look, they even wrote his name on his overalls. He's just like you, bashful."

But I won't give up. Bambi. I want Bambi!

"All right then," Mother says, finally.

I wore her out. She was already worn out. And what's more, we had to leave immediately.

I was so little then. I didn't understand what we were up against.

"You've got to understand what we're up against, baby. Or they'll take you away from me. Your mother won't be able to go on living."

We're in the airport in front of the bathroom.

"Go in and pee before we board the plane," says Mother. "I'll wait for you here."

"You come too, and wipe me."

"Do it yourself," she says. "Wipe yourself carefully. You're a big girl now. You've grown up. Leave Bambi in the bathroom. Then wash your hands and come straight back. The plane's about to take off."

"Nooo! Mommy, nooo! No, no, no! He's Bambi, my brother. He's coming to Istanbul with us. He's coming too. He's coming too!"

I sink onto the floor, in tears, Bambi on my lap. I'm kicking and beating the floor.

Sitting next to me, Mother takes my hands in hers and squeezes, hard.

"Look into my eyes," she says. "Quick, look into my eyes."

Terrified, I look.

"Do I have to slice out one of my eyes to teach you manners, is that what you want?"

She pulls something out of her back pocket. And slides it open. Something sharp: it has the sharpest blade. The sharpest blade when it's open.

"I'll slice out my eye right now. If you don't listen to me, if you won't listen to me, if you don't learn to listen to me, you'll come to your senses when I slice out my eye. When you see the blood gush— Do you remember the gushing blood?"

No, no! I don't remember gushing blood. I can't remember. Blood never gushed. I don't know how blood gushes.

Don't cut out your eye. Don't cut out your eye, Mommy. Please, don't do it, Mommy. Don't lose your eye because of me. Don't become ugly, Mommy. Don't become ugly and blind.

Sobbing, I seat Bambi on top of the toilet. I throw my arms around his neck and give him a kiss.

Good-bye, Bambi. Brother. Bambi.

Mother's taken my hand. We're racing to the gate when I pee in my pants.

I cried so much I wet myself.

Mother wipes me dry on the plane. She dresses me in clean underwear. She stuffs my wet underwear and skirt into the waste receptacle in the lavatory.

"Listen, I had so many toys. I had a playroom just for toys. I had a dressing room. They're all gone now. None of it matters, baby. Mommy was so unhappy. They made me suffer so much. I don't want any of it, I don't remember anything; I don't want to remember, either. But you'll have so many good things to remember. You can't take everything with you, that's all. Your mother will never make you suffer. I promise."

"Mommy, Mommy!" I bury my face in her neck, breathing her in as I start to cry.

"You'll have to get used to leaving things behind and running away. Or we'll get weak, feeble. We'll be dragged down. They'll catch us, they'll hunt us down. Do you understand me, baby? Are you listening carefully?"

Now I'm used to it. I got used to leaving everything behind. And I also got used to not remembering.

But I was little back then, and I cried a lot over Bambi.

Children always find something of themselves in toys. They might find their brother. And then they lose him. And then they remain in the forest. With no brother.

Not all alone, though. I have Mother.

That's all that matters. Children who are lucky aren't left in the forest without their mothers. They're always with them, always. Their mothers, only.

THE THERMAL HOTEL

I DON'T KNOW why we're at this hotel.

We're not that short of money yet.

Even later, much later, when despite mother's efforts, I realize we're running out of money, we never stay at a hotel as bad as this one.

This hotel is so upsetting it turns our stomachs. It's worse than terrible. The filth is oppressive. Sticky. Contagious.

Later, much later, we'll be forced to stay at even worse places.

But none of them have this greasy, grimy filth. This hotel is something else. Something far worse.

We're not at the seaside, we're nowhere near the sea. We're at an inland place in a thermal hotel.

I can't even swim in the pool. I try, but it's too small. I take six or seven strokes. Turn. Swim. Turn again. I'm practicing how to flip and twist into a turn.

"Very good," Mother says. "Your turns are getting a lot faster from practicing in this horrid little pool. I was never any good at turning."

Actually, Mother hated this hotel the moment we got out of the taxi and saw that hideous, broken statue at the front entrance. She was disgusted.

"Couldn't they be bothered to repair a statue that they placed themselves right at the front entrance to their own hotel?" she says in a voice that's thick with disgust. "Not only is it hideous, it's broken. Hideous and broken and right at the front entrance. How is that possible?"

This decision to come to a thermal hotel in this tedious city somewhere in the middle of the country was made in haste, in fear.

"They'll never find us here, baby. They'll never track us down. There's no way in the world they'd think of a place like this." That's what she keeps saying as we gather up all the furnishings and bedding and towels in our room.

She even gave the toilet brush to the boy she'd sent for. "Take this too, if you like. We'll replace everything today."

Pimply Boy couldn't make any sense of the hotel furnishings piled in front of the door. But he didn't make a sound. What could he say?

That same day Mother immediately bought new towels, robes, coverlets, bedspreads, and curtains. In the middle of that tedious city, turning the shops upside down.

But she found everything she wanted. Mother always finds everything she wants everywhere she goes. She even found a new toilet brush.

"We'll make do with these, baby. At least they won't foul our souls."

The instant we get back to the hotel she sends the towels, bedspreads, and sheets to the hotel laundry. Not to the dry cleaner. Dry cleaning doesn't get anything clean, as a matter of fact. It just blows filthy air.

It's a terrible problem for us. When there are no Laundromats anywhere near our hotel, Mother insists that we be allowed to use the hotel's own laundry. They advise us to use the dry-cleaning service. But Mother knows that dry cleaning doesn't do anything, as a matter of fact.

She has to teach them that too. "Let them blow that filthy air over their own clothing."

Life is hard for Mother, so tiring. I feel so sorry for her. It's a struggle, always a struggle. Teaching, forever teaching.

But the Thermal Hotel is particularly filthy and sticky, so Mother begins scrubbing the bathroom with the cleaning supplies and sponges we got at the marketplace. For ages. Until her hands are raw. Every nook and cranny.

I know how tiring it is for her. I know, because when Mother does things she doesn't want to do, she breaks her movements down into tiny fragments. And each tiny fragment of the things she doesn't want to do wears her to the bone. Even before she's begun. Cutting to the bone. She suffers so, doing things she loathes.

"Sit down and read your book, Bambi. I've got to endure this on my own."

I can't see the words through my tears. But, book in hand, I sit in an armchair over which we've draped a new purple cotton coverlet, and I pretend to read.

Without a sound. Because Mother is breaking her movements down into fragments, tens and hundreds of fragments. Breaking them apart in her head, again and again. Each fragment becoming a shard of glass. A sliver. She's suffering.

As she cleans the Filthy Thermal Hotel's bathroom—the basin, the toilet, the tiles, the floor, the mirror—she weeps softly, tears of frustration and sorrow, softly.

Me too. I'm crying too. This hotel is bad for us, Mother.

"Can we go?"

"No, baby. They'll never find us here. Believe me, we barely made it out of the Old Place. They're tracking us, breathing down our necks. I can feel their drive and their rage. Try to be patient; don't upset your mother, Bambi."

Later, we make the room our own. They've washed and pressed everything at the laundry: our new bedspreads, sheets, pillowcases, curtains, towels, bathrobes. Mother sprinkles lavender cologne over them. Now everything has been completely cleaned.

Mother can't help feeling that even the hot springs are filthy. That even the boiling-hot water might be filthy. The hot water that's bubbling up out of the ground.

We stay in the Filthy Thermal Hotel. On pins and needles. We don't want to touch anything. Mother gets us our own knives and forks and plates too. We carry them down with us to the hotel dining hall.

"You're the only one who uses the swimming pool. Getting them to change the water today wasn't easy."

We're always careful not to touch anything—in the corridors, the elevators, the dining hall. We're filled with horror and disgust. Staying here is such a struggle.

Even worse, there's nothing nearby: there's nowhere to walk, nowhere to escape from that Filthy Thermal Hotel and find shelter.

There is a garden. The hotel does have a garden full of roses, and plants and flowers whose names I don't know.

Mother gets so displeased when I ask what anything is called, the names of flowers and trees or fish. "I haven't retained anything a well-brought-up girl should know. I'll get you a new encyclopedia so you can find out whatever you want. Understand that I don't remember anything from those times. I didn't want to remember; I forgot everything."

When we're not in our room, we spread our towels on the ground in the garden and sit there. We're always the only ones in the garden.

One day Mother notices that the door to the storage shed at the far end of the garden has been left open. As we sit on our towels on the ground, she sees that the gray metal door is ajar.

"I'll have a look at that shed."

Why, Mother? But for her, a door ajar is a stain, a crack, a defect. She won't be able to return to her book unless she closes it.

Mother comes out of the shed carrying an ax. With cat steps she walks straight toward the hotel entrance.

Some people are coming out of the hotel. With the ax concealed behind her back, Mother does an imitation of a smile.

They get into their cars and drive off.

Mother begins hacking at the statue with the ax. With a vengeance. She's furious after so many days in that ugly, filthy hotel with all its defects. She's hacking with a vengeance.

That defective, broken, hideous statue is in pieces now. Mother is smiling, a real smile.

A taxi pulls up. Mother tosses the ax aside and runs toward me. Some people get out of the taxi and watch, astounded.

"Quick, to our room," Mother says.

Our backpacks are so small. We'll be ready in no time, Mother. The phone starts ringing as we leave the room.

"Let's take the stairs," Mother says. As we race down the stairs, we hear the elevator doors opening on the floor above, and shouting.

"I'll show that crazy bitch! My statue! The hotel mascot!"

Mother squeezes my hand. "Don't hear a word, baby. Shut your ears tight."

As we emerge from the hotel, a frilly woman with puffy hair and a man with a mustache, glasses, and a plastic mask of a face are getting out of a taxi. We jump in. "Quick, the bus station," Mother says. "Our bus is leaving in fifteen minutes."

And fifteen minutes later we really are on a bus pulling out of the station.

"It was hideous," Mother says. "And broken. They won't catch us, baby. Your mother is nothing like Bambi's dim-witted mother. She won't be taken in."

FAKE SOULS

WE ARRIVE AT that hotel in that little seaside town in early autumn.

The sea suddenly gets deep and rough, which is why this charming seaside town fails to draw the Horrid Hordes.

And school's started, so the beaches have emptied.

"We'll have it all to ourselves," Mother says. "The beaches will be all ours. We won't have to put up with them. Their noise, the sight of them. The overwhelmingly ugly sight of them."

And then Mother's suddenly underwater. Dragged under by sorrow and despair. As badly as she wants to surface, she can't. The Heavy-Heart Days, I know.

"Like a lump of asphalt, stuck inside me. I can't even come up for air."

The curtains are kept drawn. Mother almost never gets out of bed. She's close to tears all the time. That's why she doesn't talk much; she doesn't want to upset me.

"My heart's dragging me down, baby, down to the bottom. Hold up, it'll pass. Ignore me when I'm like this. Have patience and forgive your mother."

Every day I swim for two, two-and-a-half hours. In the sea. I gather pebbles on the beach and bring them back to our room. I show Mother the best ones, if she wants. I read in the hotel garden. I fill up my notebook.

I choose different dishes in the dining room and bring them to our room. Mother eats next to nothing. I bring her meals on an ugly tray. She doesn't even notice the imitation wood grain. She sees nothing.

But she wants me to stick to the program, to do everything on schedule. Does she even know when I enter and leave our room? I have no idea.

At Those Moments she loses all sense of time. Hours and minutes are split up into pieces: tiny fragments, excruciating partitions. Mother has no notion of the passage of time; I feel it inside.

We're both patient; we wait. She's waiting for her heart to lighten, waiting to be able to return to everyday life. I'm waiting for Mother. For her to emerge from the Heavy-Heart Days and come back.

I'm returning from the pool when I come across That Woman. "My, aren't you the prettiest little thing," she says, her eyes on mine. "Who could ever get enough of a pretty little face like yours?"

I give her a smile that's sweet. How to escape immediately?

But there is no escape. She follows me. I run into her all the time. She sits across from me while I'm having breakfast. "Are you here all alone, sweetie?"

"I'm with my mother," I say, my heart pounding in my mouth. Mother's terrified I'll speak to strangers.

But Mother's up in our room in bed all the time and That Woman doesn't look at all like one of the Snake-Tongued Bourgeois Ladies. There's something scruffy about her, and she's not at all well dressed. And she's funny and silly. I'd be ashamed to run from her.

She's small and alert, with a head of curly hair, brown and gray. And her eyes are so bright and moist, like a dog's.

"Are you Turkish? Is your mother Turkish?" She's talkative, lively. Looking directly at me with those moist doggy eyes, she asks question after question. Most I don't answer. But she doesn't mind. She asks another, or finds something else to say. A bouncy, bright dog, bounding to and fro.

She talks nonstop.

Says silly things, but I feel better.

Mother's in bed up in that dark room, unable even to open her mouth. Sometimes she pretends to read a book. But she's in no condition to read. Mother is being crushed beneath the weight of Those Moments. She's able only to breathe in, breathe out.

Talkative Woman chatters on about the weather, about this and that, about things she's seen on the television, about the hotel, about goings on and happenings and things. I feel lighter, easier. Even if her questions bother me, even if her prying scares me, she saves me from thoughts of Mother, the heavy sorrow I feel for her, overwhelmed.

That Woman does me good. She does me good during those lonely, helpless, dead-end days. She does me good and she scares me.

Mother, please don't get mad. At least she's good and open. Simple, silly. Just what I need. Try to understand me, Mother, please understand.

"Yes, we're Turkish. Mother and I. She's resting in our room; she's down with a bad case of the flu. We live abroad sometimes. I have permission from school. I'll start a little late. My father died when I was little. No, I don't miss him."

That's all I tell That Woman. Half of it isn't true, in any case.

One day Talkative Woman suggests we go to the market in town. There are such interesting shops. That's what she says.

First I say no. She says it again and again. She's been there again. She had a wonderful time. She says, always, I'm imprisoned in the hotel. Am I imprisoned? I'm what?

"Does your mother keep you imprisoned like this because you're so pretty? You're kept on a piece of string, attached to her, to your room. Why on earth can't you come to the market with me?" She keeps insisting and insisting.

"All right, we'll go one day. I'm not imprisoned, it's nothing like that. Mother's still not well. I'm worried about her."

We wander through the shops in the marketplace for ever so long. She has me try on so many clothes. And all of them look silly. But as I put them on and take them off, That Woman and the salesgirls make such a commotion, shouting and yelling, that I can't help myself, I try on everything.

"Oh my God!" That Woman shouts, clapping her hands. "I've never seen such a beautiful girl, not in my whole life."

She finally makes me take a ruffled miniskirt; a short-sleeved blouse, red, with white polka dots and a lacy collar. And white shoes, with heels. My first heels.

"I look like Minnie Mouse," I say. They don't even listen.

"You're a knockout, a real knockout."

"What? What do you mean a 'knockout'?"

Back at the hotel, I finally get away. I want to take everything off in the changing room at the pool. But she follows me.

"Hey, what are you doing? You're not ashamed of those clothes I got you, are you? Aren't you going to show your mother? Or are you afraid she'll get mad?"

"Of course I'm not. Why would she get mad?"

I'm too tired and defeated to do anything but run up to our room. Mother won't even notice. I'll change right away, in the bathroom.

The curtains are open when I walk into the room. Mother is pacing.

"Where were you?" she shouts. "I nearly died of worry. How could you do this to me?"

"Mom, nothing happened. I'm fine. You weren't well, and I was just passing the time..."

"Passing the time? What exactly is the meaning of that appalling outfit? Who dressed you up like a child prostitute? Who were you with? Where? What were you doing? Tell me immediately!"

Mother screams as she beats her head with her fists.

She's beating herself so she won't beat me; I know it.

"Mom! Stop it! Don't hurt yourself. It was a woman, just a woman. She insisted, and I went to the marketplace with her. I'll never see her again. I won't talk to her. Mommy, stop hurting yourself; stop it! Stop it!"

I rush to her side and grab her fists. Mother pulls loose and begins pounding her head against the wall. Blood gushes from her forehead. I dash into the bathroom for a towel.

"You need to be afraid of them. You need to keep them away. They're Fake Souls. They seem good and kind at first, then they start laying traps. They'll get all our secrets. They'll get us. They'll tell the whole world who we are."

Who are we, anyway? I don't know who I am.

"Take those whorish things off this instant! Right now! How could they dress you like that? She's one of them, the Fake Souls. Don't you see? Take it all off, now!"

Mother begins tearing at my blouse.

I begin to cry. What did I do? What have I done? I was lonely. I couldn't resist. Mother, I was lonely and I couldn't stand it. I'd never go near the Fake Souls; I didn't want to upset you. I didn't want to make you mad.

"Forgive me, Mom. I'll never talk with any Fake Souls again. I won't fall into their traps. Forgive me, Mom, forgive me."

Mother and I hold each other. We cry ourselves to sleep. We'll leave first thing in the morning. We'll go somewhere the Fake Souls can't get near us. Mother and I will go to a clean New Place.

THE CRAZY NUN

MOTHER AND I are in Piazzale Michelangelo. We're looking out over Florence.

Mother doesn't like Italy, not at all. But she says I have to see it.

"You have to see Italy, Bambi. Later on you won't be able to say that your mother never showed you Italy."

I won't say that, Mother. You showed me everything. Every place I had to see.

"Rome's so much nicer, in fact. But everyone's infatuated with Florence. Here you go: a bird's-eye view of Florence!"

Mother's so cheerful and full of life today. I'm a bit uneasy. I don't know why. I must not be used to it. Or it might be because she could suddenly go skidding down into Those Moments, sliding down too fast to stop.

I'll hold on to you, Mother. You've let your black hair down your back, down to your black shirt, and your black eyes are sparkling with life. You're so beautiful. The most beautiful mother in the world.

"Look, baby, look how green it is."

We walk alongside a winding road, down into the greenness. There's green everywhere, so many shades.

We are swimming through the greenery. Down we go; we've started running. I'm ahead. Mother's panting a little. She smokes so many cigarettes because she has no choice; because there's nothing else she can do, she smokes cigarettes. They're stealing Mother's breath. I hate cigarettes for stealing Mother's breath.

But we're happy, running over the green ground. We're so happy.

Then I start; I'm startled. Something is coming up the winding road, something making strange sounds, piercing cries no human or animal could possibly make. The cries bring my heart into my mouth. At the place where asphalt meets earth, I see Her.

A tiny woman in her forties. She reads my eyes, sees how stunned I am, how scared. She's reading my face.

She reads my horror and fear, and she makes a terrible face. Opening her eyes wide, she sticks out her tongue as far as she can. She wags her tongue from side to side. She rolls her eyes. The sharp, short cries become a horrible scream. A horrible scream no human could make.

I stand frozen, terrified.

This makes her even crazier. She rolls her eyes. Her tongue goes in and out, in and out. The screams go on and on. She won't stop. I'm scared. I'm so scared.

Mother catches up.

She leaps out of the green, onto the asphalt.

"Stop it! Stop it, bitch! What are you doing? Why are you scaring my daughter, you bitch?" Mother yells until her throat's torn.

"You fucking crazy bitch! How can you scare a child? A baby! How dare you scare my baby!"

The woman keeps screaming. It seemed to stop a moment when Mother jumped out. She pulled in her tongue. But her eyes are spinning around, and she's screaming. She won't stop.

"Run back up, quick!" Mother shouts to me. "Get back up there, now!"

"Mommy, Mommy!"

"Don't make me tell you again," Mother says. I race up through the greenery.

A moment ago, just a moment ago, Mother and I were so happy running through the green. I wonder where That Madwoman came from? Why'd she scare me? Why was she screaming like that? I didn't do a thing to her.

She didn't even know me. I'm not little anymore, but I'm not big either, I'm still a child. Why'd she do it? What did I do to her? Why, I wonder, why?

Choking on tears, I make it back through the greenery, back up to the top of the hill, to the place where we stepped off the road and onto the earth.

I'm back on the asphalt road, waiting for Mother.

Waiting for Mother.

Mother, what if That Madwoman does something to you? Are you OK, Mother? Are you OK? I'm so worried.

Mother holds me tight. I'm still trembling.

As she smooths back my hair, plastered to my face with tears, her hand smears my face. Her hands are dirty, the color of rust. Sticky.

She keeps wiping her hands on her jeans. "It's good I had my *falçete* with me," she says. "Thank God I had my *falçete* in my handbag. That filthy maniac! That disgusting madwoman!"

I can't stop crying; I'm gasping. "What does *falçeta* mean, Mommy?"

"*Fal-çet-e!* It's a Turkish word. The Turks, our lumpen hordes, say *falçeta*, with an *a* on the end. It makes it easier for them to pronounce. It comes from Italian: *falcetto*. Would you believe it? Italian! In English it's *knife*. Just look at your mother, burbling nonsense."

"Mommy."

I bury my nose in Mother's neck. She's talking and talking to make me forget what happened, I know. But I can't help it. I can't stop crying; I can't stop the fear, the shock, the horror; I can't stop feeling something's happened that's terribly unfair.

"I can't help it. I'm sorry, Mom. I was so scared. And I was scared she'd do something to you."

"That crazy nun?" Mother says. "That filthy thing, do something to me? That maniac?"

"She wasn't a nun," I say, sucking in my breath. "She wasn't dressed like a nun."

"They don't wear habits anymore, not all of them. My family sent me to a terrible nun school. I'd know one a mile away. Didn't you see her shoes? They were nun shoes!"

"What are nun shoes like?"

"Baby, let's get back to the hotel straightaway. Forget all about it. They're all like that: laced, heelless, stubby, freshly polished, black. Show me a thousand shoes and I'll spot the nun ones. I can smell them a mile away."

When we reach the hotel, Mother washes and washes her black shirt and her blue jeans. Then she stuffs them into a bag. She empties her handbag and puts the bag inside it. Probably her *falçete* too. Or whatever it's called. She doesn't show me.

"Go and take a shower, Bambi. Then push the Erase Button, the one in your head. When I think of how that crazy woman frightened you, I could kick her head in, even now."

I wash myself for a long time.

My tears and horror and fear won't go away. Why'd she do that? That's the question I keep asking myself; it's horribly wrong. That question. I can't get it out of my head.

She must have been crazy, just like Mother said.

But was she a nun? Would a nun do a thing like that?

Her sweater was dark blue, her shirt was beige. She had a long, dark-blue skirt. She's right in front of my eyes, still. And what she did. Especially her tongue. In and out. Worse than the screaming was that tongue and those wide-open eyes, spinning round and round.

How would Mother know a nun? How would she know her just from her shoes? Mother loves Jesus a lot. She carries a cross in her handbag. Sometimes she wears it. If that woman were a nun, wouldn't her life be dedicated to Jesus? Why would she scare me like that?

I can't forget her.

Mother told me to press the Erase Button. I have perfected the Erase Button. I press it, and nothing's left.

But have I? Why do I remember so many things; how can I remember so much?

There are some things I can't remember too, Mother. Things I don't remember at all. So many things, believe me. It's as if they're under clouds and fog, curtains, blankets. Layer after layer of blankets.

We'll leave this hotel immediately. Mother wants to leave Florence too, immediately. For us, it's become the Crazy Nun Place. It's fouled, spoiled. Destroyed.

Mother throws her bag of wet things into an airport waste bin.

We're unable to get a plane that night. We'll wait at the airport until early morning and take the first plane back to Turkey.

Some call a place home. "We have no home, no country," Mother says. "We're hotel birds. We alight on hotel after hotel. Bambi, believe me, it's better this way. They'll never catch us this way, never destroy us."

We're so happy in hotels, Mother. And we're full of joy running down through green, unless we run into Crazy Nuns.

Why are they there? Why do they find us? Why do they upset us, Mother, you and me? We don't do anything to them... Why do they upset us? Why do they hurt us?

THE TALKATIVE WOMAN

SHE WAS SITTING in the hotel garden, leaning against a tree, reading. Of course I couldn't help noticing her.

A young girl, all alone. Almost a young woman. She must have been about fourteen or fifteen. She was always wearing the most peculiar outfits, the most peculiar hats. In the most peculiar colors.

Even her swimsuit, I mean, covering her all up. She was dressed like the daughter of a conservative family or something. But like the conservative families in those old films, the foreign ones. She wasn't like us, not one bit. No, she looked just like a foreigner. Everything about her was so strange.

I assumed she was a foreigner when I first saw her. I mean, what Turkish family would leave a girl her age all alone like that all the time?

A girl like her, and was she ever a knockout. Stunning. I felt kind of funny inside just looking at her. I found myself knocking on wood. May the Lord protect her from evil, I kept repeating to myself. If I say a thing once, I say it forty-one times. You know how you have a favorite houseplant and you keep watering it, until it starts drooping from too much water? It was kind of like that. I was worried I'd hex her, give her the evil eye. She was that stunning. I couldn't keep my eyes off her. No one could. I worried myself sick over the way the others were staring at her. I worried over the evil eye.

She had this way of hanging her head and keeping it kind of tilted to one side. Those long, curly lashes, the way she looked up at you, all shy. You just melted away. Such a funny little thing. I've never seen anything like it.

Like a gazelle, lost in the forest. That's the feeling I got. Its mother ran off, or was shot by hunters, and it's been left behind, all alone in the forest. It doesn't know what to do or where to go. A beautiful gazelle. A real gazelle beauty.

You felt like picking her up in your arms and taking her home. That's exactly the feeling she gave me. A motherless kitten. She gave you such a nice, pure feeling. The little sweetie, such a sweet thing. She was so respectful. So polite you melted.

Later on I saw her at the pool, working out. That's what she called it. "I have to go and work out in the pool," she kept saying.

Back and forth, round and round, up and down. Swimming all the time in that empty hotel pool. Poor little thing.

It must have been that mother of hers making her do it.

Funny, we never got so much as a peep at the mother's face, not once. "My mother, my mother," on and on; mother this, mother that. She was obviously terrified of that mother of hers. She was terrified of something, that pretty little gazelle, the poor thing, and so pretty. You understood right away. It was impossible not to.

Just one day without swimming, you'd think; just one day without one of those peculiar hats on her head, walking along the beach for hours—fat chance. That was out of the question. Like it was an obligation, a duty.

I mean, you watch some TV, you chat a bit, you go wander around the marketplace. That's what all the girls her age do. You have a look around, check out the boys; you know what I mean?

Not on your life! It was like she was in some kind of prison. I even said as much. That girl was like a prisoner! Her mother's prisoner.

"I have to get back to our room," she kept saying. She'd carry food up to her mother, on a tray.

Even the sickest person in the world would come down to the dining room now and then, to show her face if for no other reason. I mean, what's going on, lady, are you dying up there or what? You know what I mean?

That mother kept that child of hers tied up, as though she were at the end of a short piece of string, or some bits of string. And just when it seemed she was going to talk, going to open up a little bit—bam, the string's being yanked again, from somewhere up there. She'd go all pale; "I've got to get back to our room. Mother will get worried about me," she'd keep saying.

That woman kept her child at the end of a piece of string, that's what she did. She never gave her any slack. I sensed it. Right in my gut. But I didn't say a word.

Who do I tell? Who do I complain to?

Now I'm sorry as can be. I shouldn't have let it drop. Seeing how I doted on her, seeing how sorry I felt for her, I should have raised hell.

One day I couldn't take it anymore; I twisted her arm into going shopping with me. Get the poor thing some air, I thought. We'd have a few laughs, have some fun, I'd get her to open up.

And those peculiar outfits of hers. Like she'd jumped right out of an old movie. She was such a pretty girl, the kind of girl you couldn't take your eyes off. Why not get her into some normal clothes, I thought. You know, the stuff all the other kids are wearing these days. You know what I mean?

The salesgirls went crazy over her. She looked great in everything she tried on; God himself must have been full of compliments when he was making her, I can tell you that. So I got her some white shoes, with heels. Oh, she was like something straight off the catwalk. Or one of those girls in the music videos. Even prettier, prettier than the whole lot of them. No one could hold a candle to her.

We untied that thick hair of hers, so it fell down over her shoulders. We had her walk back and forth. She was happy; she finally knew what it was to be happy. I could tell. I saw her eyes smiling.

That poor baby gazelle. Who wouldn't pity her? It was impossible not to. All alone in the forest, motherless. It was so obvious, to anyone who really looked.

She went all pale while we were still on our way back to the hotel. Her mother scared her to death; that's when I realized it, at that very moment: how badly she'd been scared and intimidated, brought up by that malicious woman.

I did my best to comfort her. "I'll go with you, to your room. I'll take the blame. I'll explain everything to your mother," I said, but it was no good, she wouldn't listen.

She didn't hear what I said. Like she was so scared a curtain came down over her eyes, covered her ears.

The first thing she did when we got back to the hotel was to tie up her hair. And she started tugging at her skirt, pulling it down. "Are you scared?" I asked her, but it didn't do a bit of good, none of it did a bit of good. She didn't even hear me. She didn't even see my face.

She ran straight to the pool. And when I rushed after her, she ran straight to her room! To her mother. The sheer terror! The mother imprisoned that girl, her own daughter.

Of course, later when I saw her picture in the papers, everything made sense.

You moron, you moron! That's what I kept saying to myself, for days on end. Why didn't I just grab her and carry her away? Why didn't I rescue her from her mother?

The least I could have done was to cause a scene. I could have kicked up a fuss, right there at the hotel. I might have been able to rescue that wounded gazelle from her mother.

You'll never believe it, but I was determined to do something the very next day, first thing in the morning. I'd made up my mind. Right before I went to sleep. I told everyone back home all about it, on the phone. They said I was right. "Do whatever you think is best," they said.

Well, what else could they say? They all know me. Once I've made up my mind, that's it, I'll burn down Rome if I have to. Oh, they all know what I'm like.

I was up at the crack of dawn, out looking for her, right down to the end of the beach. But there was no sign of her there, at breakfast, in the pool, in the garden; not a sign of her anywhere.

I was racing all over the place, like a mad cow, looking for her. Sometimes she'd hide from me. She didn't want to run into me, to spend time with me—I knew it.

But I always managed to corner her somewhere. Once we started talking, she couldn't help herself. She'd hang her head, talk in that little-girl voice, so sweet. There were times she wouldn't answer me. Acted like she couldn't hear me.

Some of my questions were too much for her; I guess I pried a bit. She'd wince and shrink. I'm no dummy, I understood perfectly well. I didn't push her. She didn't have to answer. It's not like I'm a cop or something. She could answer, or not. As she pleased.

And then it hit me. Could she have been kidnapped? I asked myself.

Next thing I know I'm at reception. I was right, of course. They'd run off first thing in the morning.

I wanted to get their surnames. Their address. Were they really Turkish, what was their background, who were they? I wanted to find out everything about them.

The guy at reception sure was a nasty piece of work. No divulging of guest information! My ass!

I went up to their floor and caught the cleaner. They'd left all the tables and nightstands and chairs out on the balcony covered in pebbles. That little gazelle was collecting them all the time.

They'd left behind a lot of clothes too. I couldn't believe it! That brand new pair of white shoes, that frilly little skirt, and the polka-dot blouse, torn.

My baby gazelle left behind the clothes I got her. That's when I knew.

There's more to this than meets the eye, I said. I knew it. I'd had my suspicions all along. But that woman, well, she's such a pro. The second she sensed I had my eye on her daughter, they beat it.

She grabbed the poor girl and whisked her away, just like that. Oh, how I wished she were mine, how I wanted her to come and live with me. I would have treated her like a regular princess. I would have given her a normal life. I would have raised her normally.

She'd be dressed just like everyone else; she'd sit and chat, get all dolled up, go out and have a good time. There'd always be a bunch of boys after her. I'd know how to handle them too, and when the time came, so long as her kismet was good, I'd know how to marry her off—

But it seems it's not to be; she was doomed to a life with that malicious mother.

My unlucky little gazelle. When I think about her, even now, I still miss her, still grieve for her. I could have saved her, but she slipped right through my fingers at the last moment.

It's too sad, too much to bear. Thinking about it now is more than I can take.

You know what I mean?

FETUS

THOSE WERE PERHAPS the best days Mother and I had together. Our days in India, in Goa.

Actually, we're always fine, happy and easy. But sometimes bad things happen to us. It's because of them. They're many, and bad.

They appear unexpectedly and bother us. They make us uneasy and leave Mother no choice but to go on the attack.

Mother doesn't want to, not at all. She doesn't want to have to protect us. "We're on the run as it is," she says. "As if that weren't bad enough. How painful that we have to protect ourselves as well, how painful!"

But there are times when we find shelter in a tiny corner of the world without anything bad happening to us. They're the most wonderful times. And Mother doesn't slide into her Heavy-Heart Days. We're not stumbling through the day every day, Mother. You're not forced to pick up the day's pieces and fragments.

We're in Arambol, at that seaside village in Goa. We have a one-room house made of cinder blocks. We open our door and step onto the sand.

We draw water from the well, to wash ourselves. We draw water to wash our clothing. We have a plastic bucket tied to a string we lower into the well. The pink and green buckets our landlady gave us have thin necks and fat bellies. Later, in the marketplace, Mother finds the old copper buckets. We get two: a little copper bucket for me and a big one for Mother. Mother gives them a name: Mother and Daughter. She does that sometimes, with toys and cockleshells, when she's in high spirits. Sometimes.

We draw water from the well in our copper buckets and wash our clothes with blue soap on the wooden plank in front of our door. Barefoot on the sand, getting soaked, washing clothes on that big plank of wood, it's so much fun!

Mother lets me wash clothes too. I'm thrilled to be in Arambol, rubbing and rubbing our thin Indian trousers, our underwear, our muslin shirts, our worn-out T-shirts, rubbing them between my hands with blue Indian soap.

We wash everything we have as often as the Indians, so often that everything's becoming thin, frayed, and translucent. Mother sits in front of our one-room house, darning holes or torn seams. "I've certainly improved as a seamstress here. Look how nicely I've mended your shirt."

Sometimes we string together the cockleshells we collected on other beaches along the Arambol coast. Hanging in the doorway of our house and from our two huge windows are hundreds and thousands of cockleshells, all in rows, on lengths of string.

Right next to our clothes-washing plank is our Cockleshell Laundry. That's what Mother calls the little plank. We wash and dry our cockleshells on it, one by one. We separate the ones with holes and string them up. So much fun!

On Wednesdays we get into a jam-packed minibus to go to Anjuna Flea Market. We need to change minibuses three whole times. It takes two-and-a-half, three hours to get to Anjuna. But the market rambling through the village forest is so amusing we go at least every other week without fail.

We get huge lapis lazuli necklaces and Kashmir work bracelets. We get vests and skirts with tiny mirrors from Rajasthan, even if we know we'll never wear them.

We get enormous cotton backpacks embroidered with mirror work and bird designs. "We're like birds too," Mother says. "Full of life, and free. Aren't we, Bambi?"

Yes, Mother. In Goa, in this slice of time, for more than in a long time, we're happy and in high spirits.

Fetus appears at our front door one day. A dog, tiny and dirty white, his belly bloated from hunger. With his pointy ears too big for his face, he's adorable! I can't resist taking him onto my lap the moment I see him. "Mommy, can we keep him?"

"That's the ugliest thing I've seen in my entire life!" Mother laughs. Mother loves him too. She wants him, I can tell from her voice.

"He looks like an alien. Can we call him Alien?"

"Let's call him Fetus," Mother says. "When I was in primary school they took us to the Red Crescent dispensary, next door to the school. There were fetuses in jars labeled three months, five months, and six months. My classmates were so horrified they didn't know what to do. It was years before they got over those fetuses displayed in jars. They had nightmares about them."

I don't pay any attention to Mother's horror story. Mother has named our puppy. He's ours. We have a dog now! I get to keep Fetus.

"He's every bit as ugly as the fetuses in those jars. But we'll take care of him until he's in better shape."

With Fetus still on my lap, I hug Mother. She doesn't know what to do with her arms and hands. She gets stiff when I hug her if she hasn't put her arms around me first.

We make a collar for Fetus out of a nice cloth necklace we got in Anjuna. We bathe him again and again. We sprinkle him with flea powder. He's the cleanest puppy in the world. Sometimes I wrap him in a towel and settle him between my legs, rocking him back and forth, like a baby. He grins a dog grin at me. He's so quick and understanding.

Sometimes we get milk and bread from the little shop next to Rosebud Bar. There isn't any dog food, of course. We bring back leftovers from restaurants and mash them up good in his bowl. We give him eggshells for vitamins.

Fetus is so hungry, so hungry for love. Mother doesn't want him coming down to the beach with us. He'll be hot and sad if he has to bake in the sun for hours. But we have to look after him.

He always follows us anyway, as we're walking along the beach. We try hiding in a clump of bushes so he can't find us. Sometimes we yell at him to go home.

But my little Fetus is so quick. He always finds us. His long, skinny tail is wagging and wagging, he's so happy. I can't help hugging him.

"I'll carry him in my arms, Mom. He'll wait for us in the shade, under a tree."

Mother smiles. She smiles.

I've never seen anyone smile as beautifully as my mother.

She doesn't pick up Fetus. "I'm glad he's not totally white. At least he's not pure white and furry."

Mother, I know you have a problem with white dogs. I know about that terrible nightmare. Fetus is only a puppy. He's still a baby, tiny and hairless. No one would do anything to him. He needs us. And I need him so much. I'm thrilled to be with him, thrilled to be able to take care of him.

"Let's stay here forever, Mom, in Arambol. Why don't we make our home here?"

"We can't stay here, baby. We can't stay here any longer than we can stay anywhere else. They'll get wind of us, find us, track us down. You're my home, and I'm your home. We can't stay anywhere forever."

"Who are they, Mom? Why are they following us? What did we do to them? What do they want to do to you?"

Mother smiles. I'm hurting her, I know. But here in Arambol, Mother's become softer. We're sitting in a bamboo restaurant overlooking the ocean, eating fried shark, drinking lassi.

"Look at the ocean, the beauty. Dark blue into eternity. Finish up your plate, Bambi. Shark's quite good, isn't it? We've really gotten used to it here, haven't we?"

We've gotten used to it, Mother. I always get used to it. I like life. My home, my country, my world, my ocean; you're all of them.

"Fetus is getting sad all alone. Come on, let's go back home."

"That's not home. We don't have a home. Bambi, we'll be leaving this place soon. When the time comes, you won't get upset and make me regret having let you keep Fetus, will you? You're my big girl, clever as can be. I can depend on you right to the end, can't I, baby?"

You can depend on me, Mother. There won't be a single tear in my eye when we leave Fetus and go. I won't make you regret having let me look after him and love him.

But I'll feel like I'm splitting up inside. I'll feel a sadness inside, welling, swelling, first in my eyes and nose, then down. I'll be under a heavy grief I've never known.

I'll feel all of this and I won't let you feel any of it.

Crying, curled up with longing, I'll wake up for weeks to the sound of Fetus.

"Well done, baby," you'll say, squeezing my hand in the Bombay airport. "This is how you must be. Always prepared to leave everything behind at a moment's notice. It's essential, for the two of us to stay alive. So they don't take you from me. If they take you from me, I couldn't go on living. Thank you, baby. Thank you so much. You're my strong and clever Bambi."

THE MOTHER CROW

"OUR HOUSE WAS reached either by climbing up one of those curious steep streets of stairs," Mother says, "or by winding round through the back streets. I'd always climb up that street made of steps, out of breath. Already out of breath, fearing that place called home. My heart was already pounding in my mouth; how will Mother provoke a quarrel today, how will she torment me, how will I be wounded, inside and out?"

Mother's forgotten everything in her past. "I've even forgotten what I've forgotten," she says, again and again.

But then there are those times—a crow, a sign of some kind—and Mother's suddenly dragged back into her past. Her voice changes, and so does the color of her eyes. The light goes out, they become dull. Her voice becomes tangled, knotted. That beautiful scratchy voice is gone. Replaced by a square thing. Her voice chopped, in tiny squares.

The Past-Time Voice is what I call it. Cut short. Muffled.

She begins. Not for long. But not briefly, either. She describes her past. How she feared and how she was frightened.

"I haven't got a past anymore, Bambi. And nobody from my past; they've all disappeared. But I still can't help fearing that they'll spring out of a well or a hole and drag me back. Fear's like that. Once it's permeated your soul, just once, it'll suddenly sink in its claws yet again at the most unexpected moments. The stains of fear never come out, they just grow and grow, all on their own."

Walking along the shore, we see a crow. Jet black. Crow black. I know Mother loves crows. One time a walnut fell out of a crow's beak and onto Mother's head. "You silly little rascal you; if it's actually true that you're the smartest of birds, surely you can do better than that," she said, laughing and laughing.

But this crow, the crow we chance upon out walking, descends on Mother like an ominous cloud. Sweeping Mother back into her Past-Time Voice.

"One day, as I ran up those steps, running up those steps just to be out of breath, I saw a baby crow. Something was wrong with its wing. It was lying on a step, in the corner, its breast rising and falling, breathing hard. I crouched down to see what had happened to the poor thing. I'd just crouched when the mother crow—she must have been there somewhere, hovering, making sure nothing hurt her baby—she swooped down into my hair. I didn't know what hit me! I sprang up from the ground and kept running up the stairs, all the way. To the house with Mother, where I was even less protected than that baby crow. To the house of Mother, who didn't, couldn't love me as much as that mother crow loved her baby. I was crying. Breathless."

Mom, you're breathless now too. You're crying too. You're talking in your Past-Time Voice. You're pulling me close with one arm. I'm resting my head on your breast. Wave after wave of Mother Smell is enveloping me.

"Your grandmother's dead now. The only motherly thing she ever did was to die young. It's because of her money that we're able to live like this. We're eating away at her money. Your mother's squandering her inheritance! A rat, gnawing away at Mother's money! My mother's money; she was never a mother."

Mother smiles. I relax. And her Past-Time Voice is gone. It finally left us, cleared out.

"You mean I don't have a grandmother?"

"You don't, Bambi. She died before you were born. She wasn't able to see you. She couldn't mark you out for misfortune."

"If I don't have a grandmother, who are we running from? Is your father after us? Is my father? Who are we running away from, Mother?"

"I feared every letter that came into that house. Feared every ring of the phone and ring of the doorbell. Fear, every time Mother opened a door or shut it. Every time I heard water running in the bathroom. But more than anything, I feared the sound of her footsteps.

"The *crack, crack* of her heeled slippers coming toward my room. In front of my door, she would shout, 'How many times have I told you not to shut this door!' I feared that horrible voice; what I heard in it was the coldness of wealth, the cruelty of power—I was so afraid in that house, of everything. I was so afraid of everything about Mother and Father that I became fearless about everything else!"

Mother has slipped back again. If only I hadn't asked, hadn't insisted, hadn't pushed, Mother wouldn't have slipped back into that ominous Past-Time Voice.

You stupid child! You haven't grown up. You've failed to grow up. You're still upsetting your mother. I'm so furious at myself for having been so thoughtless. I start biting my lower lip.

Mother hates it when I bite my lower lip. But I can't stop myself; I sink my teeth in, harder.

Suddenly blood gushes.

Blood's dripping onto my baby-blue shirt. As I wipe the stain with my hand, it grows bigger. The more I wipe it, the bigger it gets, like Mother's Fear Stain.

"Baby! Baby!" Mother's seen. She's seen my mouth. Seen my bloody lower lip. Seen the stain on my new shirt. She's seen the stain smear and grow. She's seen it. Even though I've stood up, I've turned my back. I was going to go into the sea so she wouldn't see. I was going to sink in up to my neck.

Mother's taken me in her arms, holding tight.

We hold each other tight. Now we're crying.

"Forgive me. Please forgive me. Forgive me for my past. Forgive me for failing to escape my past, Bambi. Forgive your mother."

"Mommy, I love you so much," I sob. I'm sobbing so hard I'm choking. I can't breathe. How did we get to this place? How did we sink down to this place? Just now when we were doing so well.

"It's all so you won't have to go through what I did. It's all so they don't get you, Bambi. Forgive me, and please don't keep on at me."

"I won't. I'm sorry. I'm sorry if I broke your heart, Mommy. If I reminded you of your past, I'm so, so sorry." I'm sobbing too hard to get out the words.

Mother washes my face with water from the sea. We toss the bloody baby-blue shirt into the water. I'm in an undershirt. And I don't mind. Mother takes off her sweater. She helps me put it on.

We're lying on the pebbles.

It's cold. We hold each other tight. I want my sobs to stop. But they don't.

I want us to be Fine Again. I want us to be Fine Again. The way we were before the crow. The way we were at the fish restaurant. The way we were before we went for a walk.

Now we're lying on the pebbles clinging to each other and things are bad. So bad. But soon the waves will come and carry away the sadness inside. We'll be Fine Again.

We'll get up and go back to the hotel, Mother.

We love this hotel and this seaside village. It's our third time. We've never been to any hotel more than twice. And never a second time to the ones that are bad for us. We never go back. We never set foot in the ones we run from.

In the hotel, Mother says, "We're a Moon Unit, Bambi. We're all we need. They are many, and bad. We won't be deceived. Believe me; always know that I've done what's right and said what's right."

"They are many, and bad, Mommy. We're a Moon Unit. We're all we need."

"My darling Bambi. I stayed alive because you were born. I'm living so they won't get you, my beautiful baby."

Then Mother combs and combs my hair. I drink the soy milk we got at the market this morning. She watches me fall asleep. She'll go to sleep after me.

Sometimes she does that. Waits for me to fall asleep.

I fall asleep at once. Tired of crying. I sleep.

THE GOLDEN-HAIRED BOY

Time passed, and Bambi was learning how good the meadow grass tasted, how tender and sweet the leaf buds and the clover were. When he nestled against his mother for comfort, it often happened that she pushed him away.

"You aren't a little baby anymore," she would say. Sometimes she even said abruptly, "Go away and let me be." It even happened that his mother got up in the little forest glade, got up in the middle of the day, and went off without noticing whether Bambi was following her or not. At times it seemed, when they were wandering down the familiar paths, as if his mother did not want to notice whether Bambi was behind her or was trailing after.

One day his mother was gone. Bambi did not know how such a thing could be possible; he could not figure it out. But his mother was gone, and for the first time Bambi was left alone.

THOSE WERE STILL the times when Mother read Bambi to me in her creaky, croaky voice. I must have been little. In the South, at that wonderful hotel, in an enormous bed shrouded under mosquito netting. Mother holding me close with her arm.

Soon Mother is unable to endure Bambi's mother, and she goes out onto the terrace to smoke a cigarette. She breathes the cigarette in quickly, and just as quickly breathes it out. Mother doesn't smoke cigarettes; she eats them. That's what it looks like to me. Watching from afar.

Mother can't bear Bambi's mother: her incomprehension, her bewilderment. Her laziness. Mother can't bear how much she concerns herself with things other than Bambi.

"Don't get mad at her, Mommy. She loves Bambi a lot. She'll be sorry later."

I bound out onto the terrace, to Mother. This is a one-story hotel with rows and rows of rooms. They all have terraces opening onto a huge communal garden. Full of roving peacocks, geese, ducks, pheasants.

Whenever a male peacock fans its tail, I clap my hands in delight. They're so magical, so exquisite. Rainbow is what Mother and I call them. We call them Rainbow Birds.

"There are beautiful things in life too, Bambi. Like the peacocks fanning their tails. Like a rainbow after the rain. Do you remember Alleppey, how we walked and walked under the rainbow, along the canal? Followed by all those Indian children, do you remember? You were still so young. I carried you on my back, all the way back; you'd fallen asleep."

I remember, Mommy. I remember all the good things. I remember them the best. Those moments of happiness they tried to take from us, our best moments. I'm saving them all up. Continually, still.

"Come on, let's go for a swim, Bambi," Mother says. "The harmful rays of the sun won't burn us anymore."

"But Bambi was a boy! Why are you calling that girl Bambi?" he bellows. From the far end of our terrace. A boy! My age, my height.

Mother's speechless. Where did he pop out from, this Golden-Haired Boy? How long has he been listening to us? And he's so adorable that she can't get angry. I see it in her face. Mother can't get angry, not with him.

"We're staying next door!" he bellows. "Right next to you!" Then he walks across our terrace and stands directly in front of me. "Do you want to play?"

I've never played with children. I've seen other children, when Mother takes me to parks and zoos and carnivals. They've run up to me, on the beach, in hotel restaurants.

But those are the times when Mother's face changes. I know she's upset, and she's getting worse. I run away from those children. Just as I'm not to go to school, I know that I'm not to speak to other children, not supposed to play with them. Mother will get upset. She'll be unhappy.

And we have to escape. We're different. I've known it right from the start. Mother taught me. I'm not used to children.

"Their mothers and fathers will get involved," Mother says. "You know about our special circumstances, Bambi. We have to get away from them. They are many, and bad. But we're a unit, a unit of two."

We're a Moon Unit. Mother and me. We don't need anyone else. Or other children.

But this boy bounced into our life like a ball of light. The very moment he stepped onto our terrace, he started talking to me, playing with me.

Mother doesn't say a word. I search her eyes. They tell me nothing. So, she can't resist Golden-Haired Boy either. Those eyes, turned up at the edges, enormous and blue, are fixed on Mother's eyes as he asks question after question. He talks all the time. Full of joy and wonder.

"But isn't Bambi a boy, Auntie?" That's what he says every time Mother calls me Bambi. Mother smiles. She laughs.

"You're right," she says. "Bambi's a boy deer. But I call my daughter that too. Because we love that story. When you love something, you make exceptions."

"What's 'expection'?"

"Exception!" I scream. I know all the words, because of Mother. I know her Turkish, and I know her English. But sometimes they can't understand what she's saying. They don't know the words she uses. I do. I've always known. I use them.

They live in Canada. The boy's father is a computer programmer; his mother doesn't work. Golden-Haired Boy is talking. They have a big dog. Right now the neighbors are taking care of their big dog, because his dad comes home late. "Aunt Emily, she's taking care of Remzi right now."

Remzi is his grandpa's name; at first his mom said he couldn't name his dog Remzi too. "But I love Grandpa. So I can give his name to my dog too, because I love him too. Right, Auntie? Like Bambi!"

Mother smiles. She laughs. I laugh too. The three of us are happy, Mother. Golden-Haired Boy isn't one of them. He brings us joy.

His mother and aunt are on vacation. He's forever running from them and to us. We're together almost all the time. At the foot of a mountain in this hotel of peacocks. We're as happy as if we found ourselves under a rainbow after the rain.

One day, Golden-Haired Boy brings over a book. He wants to give it to me. It's a book called *Thomas the Tank Engine*; it's full of big pictures, but not many words.

I could cry I'm so excited. It's the first time, the very first time, someone gave me a present, someone other than Mother. Golden-Haired Boy is giving me his favorite book! Giving it to me.

One day, around sunset, after eyeing us only from a distance, Golden-Haired Boy's mother appears on our terrace. "I'm not disturbing you, am I? I've been meaning to ask if you minded, but he never gave me the chance. And when you didn't say anything—"

"Not at all," Mother says. "We both love him, and we enjoy his visits. He gets along well with my daughter."

"That's my little boy; oh, I can't tell you the way he makes friends with everyone, just like that. We're thinking about going into town tonight, to that meatball place. What do you say we take Bambi along too? He's been pestering me something awful, she just has to come too! I'd invite you too, but I don't think you'd like it." Laughing sounds come out of her, from all over. Even from her nose, I suppose. But her eyes aren't laughing, not at all.

Mother's body is tense as a bow. Her face is bewildered. But she's trying not to show it. Mother, I know how upset you are. I know how badly they're hurting you, Mom.

"You're right, I have no desire to go to a meatball restaurant. It'd be better if my daughter didn't go either. She's accustomed to going to sleep early."

Mother's fidgeting with a glass jug resting on the table on the terrace. I see how difficult this is for her. She's like a wire being drawn tighter and tighter.

"What difference does it make if your dear little Bambi goes to bed late one night? Come on, let her go with us! We won't eat your precious little girl, promise." She's making laughing noises again. And showing her gums. She has a face like a rodent.

"My daughter's name is not Bambi! And she can't go to that *köfte* place with you!" Mother's unable to hold herself back any longer. Her voice shoots out like a hundred arrows. The jug tips over on the table. But it doesn't break much. Only into three or four pieces. It didn't break much, Mother. We'll pick them all up.

The woman's face has suddenly turned dark red. She grabs Golden-Haired Boy by the arm and they're gone, back to their room next door.

"Is she crazy or what!" she shouts to her sister. "She practically bit my head off, the lunatic! Bambi this, Bambi that; that's all we've been hearing, for days, right? She deliberately broke that jug. I swear she did it on purpose. What a weirdo!"

Her voice rings out, sharply and clearly. Unleashing everything she couldn't say directly to Mother's face, attacking from the terrace. She wants us to hear. To be poisoned.

I carried that book with me for weeks and months. *Thomas the Tank Engine;* the sideways glance of those black eyes, that innocent smile. The book fell to pieces. So I crammed a few pages into my bags. Later, those pages fell to pieces. They disintegrated and were gone.

Golden-Haired Boy became my phantom childhood friend.

But his voice still rings in my ears. The voice of a child whose joy and goodness hasn't yet been snuffed out.

"But isn't Bambi a boy, Auntie?"

MADAM MANAGERESS

OUR MONEY IS running short. Running out. Melting away. Evaporating.

"Don't worry, Bambi," Mother says. But I know all about that ever-present feeling, somewhere in the back of her mind, somewhere in a corner of her soul: That Going-Under Feeling, that Sinking Feeling. Of failure, desperation.

"I can't bear for us to lose our comforts, your comforts," Mother says. "But our money's melting away like ice. Your grandmother had some pet sayings. She had platitudes that turned my stomach. 'A penny spared is a penny saved,' she'd say. Well, the hateful witch was right about that. I'm afraid we've come to the end of that never-ending fortune of hers. Now we'll have to find money somewhere else, Bambi."

If I have a terrible dream in the middle of the night, or wake up shivering, or wake up feeling all alone, I find Mother out on the balcony smoking a cigarette. I find her sitting in the middle of a cloud of smoke.

She can't sleep. I know she's worried we'll run out of money completely. That Sinking Feeling is keeping her up at night, tearing at her sleep.

She keeps blaming herself. She says she's mismanaged our money. "As soon as she died, I sold everything, I let it all go. I should have kept the properties. It would have been wise to live off the rent, to manage her money better. But all I wanted was to get out of her country, to be rid of her and her possessions. I didn't want us to spend our lives bickering with tenants, like her. And we had no other choice, Bambi. We had to bring the money with us, so we could keep running. I didn't want us to have to deal with other people. More than anything, I wanted us to be free of them all."

Don't worry, Mother. See, I'm all grown up now. I can look after you and myself. I can get a job. I can find work.

But what can I do, really? I'm astonished at my despair triggered by these thoughts. I worry just like Mother. I'm as upset as she is. Sinking Feeling is contagious. It oozes and trickles, coiling inside me.

But I have no right to get so upset. If Mother sees how upset I am, she'll worry even more. She'll run through more money; it will melt away even faster. Mother will grow sadder, crushed, she'll fade away before my eyes.

"I have no concept of money," Mother says. "We're spending so much because we have to get away, baby."

I know, Mother. We're replacing everything, and buying it all again. We've been staying on forsaken stretches of the coast, in strange hotels. Hotels are expensive; travel is expensive. We look for the cheapest plane tickets, but we don't always get them; we have to settle for whatever we can find when we need to escape. We have no choice, Mother. None.

"I didn't want you to learn the meaning of the word expensive. I didn't want you to have feelings of any kind when it came to money. That witch, your grandmother, tormented me, every moment of my childhood and youth, with her talk of money. She poisoned me. Incessant talk of money, in the garden, at the dinner table, in the living room, on the veranda. She and Father and their endless talk of money. I'm still nauseated by it. Even now, I can see Mother and Father, like a scene from a bad film. An inexorably, unspeakably bad film."

Mother's jittery this morning. She smokes and drinks coffee, one after another. We need to go to the bank. We need to deal with one of Them.

But we're not used to Them.

Whenever we need to go to the bank, Mother becomes jittery and irritable. That's why she withdraws such large amounts, large enough for us to live for months, without having to see their faces again.

"Let me show you to the manageress's office," says the bank teller when he sees the figure in Mother's bankbook.

The manageress is in her room drinking coffee with two other women, all equally painted, all wearing the same shade of lipstick. As though when they woke up in the morning they dipped the tips of their fingers into bowls of blood they smeared onto their lips. Their hair's piled high, streaked yellow: ugly frames for their dark complexions.

"Just look at their mouths, their lips pursed and twisted, right and left!" Mother says. And their eyebrows are inevitably tweezed into high arches. They're like the most hideous specimens of a tribe. As unchanging in their cruelty as they are in their choice of cosmetics.

"Welcome. What can I do for you?" says Madam Manageress. Our presence in her room is unwelcome; her tone flings that fact into our faces. She's managed to raise a single eyebrow high into the center of her forehead. By what right have we trespassed? What are we doing here?

"We can wait outside for your conversation to finish," Mother says. "Perhaps you want to handle our business later?"

Madam Manageress's clients are as alike as blood sisters, their mouths contorted by disapproval.

"This savings deposit has not yet matured," frowns Madam Manageress, tapping the bankbook with her nails the color of her lips.

We don't deserve to be in her room. We're different, even if we do have money.

"I know," says Mother. "But I'd like to withdraw the entire amount today, in order not to set foot in a bank again for a very long time."

"It's a considerable sum," protests Madam Manageress. We're still standing; the sisters are still sipping coffee. In silence, they conspire to expel us from the room. They purse their lips. Their first impression of Mother has not been favorable. They don't like her: her clothing, her voice, her Turkish, her simmering rage. Mother isn't one of them. She's unsettling.

"We were directed to your office. Any one of your bank clerks could have completed this transaction without delay. But never mind that, just keep sipping your blood-coffee with your blood sisters."

"Excuse me?" says Madam Manageress. The Blood Sisters are now abuzz. They don't approve of Mother, no, not one bit.

"You heard what I said," Mother says, raising her voice.

The Blood Sisters beat a hasty retreat. Although they don't even pause to kiss the air good-bye, they do manage, with their widened eyes and raised brows, to express solidarity with Madam Manageress.

"Perhaps you don't understand," says Madam Manageress, her voice growing shrill. "By withdrawing the remainder of your account today, you'll be losing a substantial amount of interest, madam!"

"It's you who doesn't understand," says Mother, leaving me by the door as she strides right up to the desk. "The money is mine, the maturity date is mine, and the interest, lost or gained, is mine."

"You're required to give us two days' advance notice," says Madam Manageress, dissolving into rage. "We don't keep sums that large in this branch."

"I'm certain you have that much money at your branch. Furthermore, I phoned in the amount two days ago. It is true, however, that I didn't leave my name."

"It was all done without my knowledge," Madam Manageress pants. "You should have notified me personally by telephone, madam."

"You're doing this because I spoiled your morning coffee, aren't you?" Mother asks. "You're making things difficult for me because I interrupted your gossip session with your blood sisters." She begins to pound her fist on the desk. Harder and harder.

Mother spins round and gives me a look. I know that look: Close the door behind you and get outside, quick, it says. Whatever happens happens, it says. Don't listen, don't know, lower your shutters.

I hate Madam Manageress, hate her for upsetting Mother, hate that ugly bloodred mouth spewing poison.

They're everywhere. They upset us all the time. It's as if their rudeness squeezes our souls and breaks our hearts.

I don't hear the sounds coming from inside the room. I've closed the door, quickly. I didn't see anything, I didn't hear anything. Just like you wanted.

Mother comes out of Madam Manageress's room. "Let's get out of this bank, Bambi," she says. "We'll get the money from another branch."

The wail of a siren grows louder as we reach the end of the street; an ambulance is racing toward the bank.

"Something must have happened to Madam Manageress," says Mother, turning to look.

"I remember how refreshed I'd feel every time I heard an ambulance, thinking they were coming to get your grandmother. So relieved that maybe she'd be out of my life. It's a wearing sound, but strangely comforting: the indifferent shriek of an ambulance carrying evil off to the darkness, where it belongs, forever."

FLOOR ATTENDANT

WE'VE GOT THESE jackets, dark red—maroon, they call it—made of this crappy, itchy fabric. Thank God they let us wear black jeans under them.

Anyway, that's my uniform.

And my job comes with a title too: floor attendant.

Floor attendant, my ass; that's what I say to myself all the time. A shitty floor attendant!

I'm trying to save up tips. Maybe then I can get away, go to Greece or something. The life I have here isn't what I'd call a life.

I mean, if you've got money you can live it up. That's what they do at our hotel.

But for guys like me, living here's like living in a dog's asshole.

My mom's always going at me, "Watch your mouth, son. You didn't used to talk dirty!" she says.

Hey, I was just a kid back then. I didn't realize life would turn out so shitty. What does it matter, anyway, in this dog-asshole job of mine? It doesn't matter if you're the best around, it's all the same. You're just a floor attendant, and that's that.

Clean up after everyone. Carry their things. Run here and there. The only good thing about it is the tips. That's the only thing that counts. Imagine that.

So when that woman and girl showed up, it was just going on winter. But it wasn't winter yet. It was a couple of months before we'd be closing for the season. We didn't have many guests. The off-season, they call it. The awful season! A few rich Russians, stuck-up old ladies. And their cheap husbands, there for the weekend.

Those old ladies would play cards all day. Canasta, I think they call it; they're all crazy about it. They'd park their asses at the card table all day long.

The girl's mother was nothing like them. She wasn't like anyone I've ever seen. There was something funny about her.

There was something funny about the girl too. But man, was she pretty!

Here I am talking about her like she's dead or something. Man, is she pretty!

Everyone was talking about her. All this talk about how they've never seen anyone so beautiful. And we get all kinds of girls here, even foreigners and high-society types.

I'll tell you what it was about that girl: you couldn't place her. You know what I mean? She stood out. The place is always crawling with those spoiled, screechy girls, all of them the same.

But then comes this girl, like out of a bedtime story, like Snow White. Or Sleeping Beauty.

A girl straight out of a fairy tale! And she stepped into our lives, into real life, and honored us.

Sleeping Beauty, that's it, perfect. And she really did look like she was half-asleep. Like half of her mind was somewhere else. Like she was sad, except that wasn't it either. It seemed she was in the middle of a dream, but walking around. A dream, the world: it was all the same to her.

And man, could she ever swim! The guys at the pool were always going on about it, what a swimmer that girl was. I found a moment, real early one morning, to watch her.

The mother spotted me, of course, looked at me something evil. I mean, that woman was the master of evil looks! You'd be turned to stone under that look. Or burned to cinders! I don't know how she did it.

Actually, she wasn't all that bad. She looked like she'd just left a funeral, is all. Like her face had fallen. Not that she was teary-eyed or anything. No, it was something else.

The girl was the same. It was like the two of them had fallen into a well, were at the bottom of a well, all alone. And no matter how loud they shouted, no one would ever hear. And no matter how bad they wanted to get out, they couldn't. That's what they were like.

And their room, what they did to that hotel room. The cleaners told us about it. They'd turned it into something else; that's what they said.

After they left—hightailed it out of here in the middle of the night—the next morning the cleaners called me in to show me.

It was jam-packed with stuff. New lamps, new bedspreads. Pebbles all over the place. Even some tree branches. They'd created this strange room. It didn't belong to the hotel anymore; it was theirs and theirs alone.

When I first saw it, I thought to myself, I hope they're not devil worshippers. I mean, the woman, Sleeping Beauty's mother, was always dressed in black. Her shirts, her jeans, those funny shoes of hers—all black.

Don't get carried away, I said to myself. It's not the devil they're in trouble with, it's themselves.

Like I said, they're in this well, trapped. And they can't talk to anyone, hang out with anyone, reach out to anyone. They're alone. Mother and daughter, all alone.

Later, I read in the newspaper about what happened, what Sleeping Beauty's mother had been up to all these years, that she's a real psycho, and no one had any idea, and on and on—

Would you have thought that woman had it in her? Well, yeah, I guess you would. There was something superstrange about the way she looked and acted. There's no denying that.

But that woman, the mother I mean, was good with the tips. Real generous. So what if she never smiled, what's it to me? Take those other ones, those grinning idiots, what good ever came of them? Better not to smile but to be a real person! Take an interest. Notice others.

She was a real person. She never set out to hurt anyone. Of course, they laughed at me later when I said that. She left a trail of destruction everywhere she went, they said.

It's a funny world we live in. Everything's wacko. And not just here in our country. I get the chance to talk to a lot of tourists; it's the same everywhere.

Some of us get stepped on and some of us get burned by the rude people, by the cheats.

Well, that woman got burned. I can't help thinking she got burned, and she's fighting fire with fire, burning them right back. What I mean to say is she's got to have her reasons for doing what's she's done. That's what I think.

"What kind of a sicko are you, anyway?" everybody said, jumping all over me for supposedly sticking up for that woman. "Fell for the girl, did you, lost your head over her, did you?" And on and on they went.

It's true about the girl; we all fell for her, everyone at the hotel.

No, no that's not true; we didn't fall for her.

Everything about them was so strange, so different.

Like they'd been beamed in. Like they were never really here, in our world; they couldn't have been. It was like they were in pain or, at the least, fed up with the whole thing. Like they were fighting for their lives.

At the bottom of a well, as I said before. They made you think things like that, a million thoughts, and not one of them normal. Not one.

And that's why you couldn't feel close to them. I mean, not one of us got fresh with the girl. How could we?

We just watched them, like a film. A foreign film. From a country we knew nothing about; it was a story we knew nothing about. And we didn't get it, not one bit.

They'd go on long walks, wander along the seaside for hours. Locked into their own little world, both outside and inside the hotel. Even inside this piece-of-shit hotel!

They say that girl spent her whole life in hotels. Her whole life! Never had a home. Forever running, here and there!

Isn't that just the strangest thing, I thought to myself, later: it's a kind of life sentence. Maybe it's because I work in a hotel, but even if hotels are fancy—with great views and beaches and swimming pools and all that—well, they're still a prison. And that's when I froze, when I thought to myself, you can run, but you can't get away; there's no escape from sameness and trouble.

And once I got to thinking—I'm one of those guys, the old brain starts racing full speed ahead once it's warmed up—I could see that the world, life, the whole shebang, well, it all adds up to one big prison cell.

It doesn't matter if you're in a hotel or at home. You're a prisoner, you're a prisoner, and that's that.

And I guess that's how the mother felt. So she made her own prison, for herself and her daughter. It's a terrible thing to do, of course. But if you've already decided there's no escape, you wouldn't see it that way, you wouldn't think you've taken someone else prisoner. You'd think you were protecting her, keeping her safe from a terrible world.

But what's done is done. And all our talk is empty, and we can all point our fingers. But it's a crying shame, when you look at what does pass for normal these days. I mean, it's all such a big mess, isn't it?

THE VACANT LOT

I KNOW HOW terrified Mother is of that city. Istanbul.

From the moment we touch the runway until we transfer to planes that take us to other airports in other cities, I know that Mother is breathing hard, clutched by claws of fear.

"Fear of fear," Mother says, "like the Fassbinder film. It's not so much the fear this city fills me with, it's the fear of fear itself. It's the fear of finding myself in a blind alley—the uneasiness, the sense of dread I thought I'd left behind long ago."

The uneasiness Mother feels is different; her restlessness is different. This city fills her with a sense of horror unlike anything else. That's what Mother tells me.

Mother doesn't hide her feelings. She can't. She always tells me everything that's going through her heart and mind. But I've never been able to understand how she can tell me so much while keeping so much from me.

"But Mother, tell me everything."

"Bambi, there are some things I don't tell you so I don't fall to pieces. So I can pull myself together. We have to stay in one piece to get away from them, you know that."

This time, we aren't leaving the city immediately. It's a gentle autumn day.

"Come on," Mother says, "I'll show you Karaköy and Eminönü."

She says they're wonderful places. The best places in Istanbul, the real Istanbul.

"They're the liveliest places in the city, places where life is lived. And when you're there, you can hear it, the heartbeat of Istanbul. And you know that you too must live. You feel the vitality and beauty of a beating heart."

But when we get into the taxi, she tells the driver a different place: "Bebek," she says. "I'll give you directions when we get closer."

Mother's eyes are going glassy, are turning into eyes of glass. Mother's terrified, I know. She fears fear. Fear of the fear she felt and will feel here, in the Mother City. Fear of the freshness of old fears.

She begins to give the driver directions.

"Mother, are we going to the stairs where the Mother Crow attacked you?"

"No. We're going to a vacant lot. To the vacant lot of my childhood."

The taxi pulls into a dead-end street. We get out at the Vacant Lot.

It's like a little box, with an open square in front, but closed in on the other three sides by rocky hillsides. A box whose front has been torn open.

When you step inside, you're in a box of earth and rock. A box with a view.

From the open front, you can see the Bosphorus.

"Look, you can see Bebek Bay from here," Mother says. "We won't go to the stairs where the crow attacked me. They lead to our house. To mother's house, to horror."

Mother tells me, for the first time, about a white dog she had as a child, a noisy, crazy dog.

"It barked all the time; it was the most protective, jumpiest dog you'll ever see. A mad dog, and I loved it all the more because it was unhappy and imperfect. The less Mother and Father loved it, the more attached I became. It couldn't help it; it was just ill-tempered, unbalanced. It was terrified of everything. That's why it was so aggressive: whether it had a reason or not, it was utterly terrified."

Mother sinks down onto a boulder overlooking the Bosphorus. She's taken a turn for the worse. Her voice has changed. First her eyes changed, then her voice. Her voice has shattered into pieces. Slivers.

"Mommy, what happened to the dog?"

"Father's driver buried it right over there, under that hornbeam tree. He was father's helper and did all his dirty work for him. I still can't handle anyone who looks like him. Even now, if I see someone with those hands, or those eyes, I know I'm going to have a bad day."

"Mommy, what happened to the dog?"

"They couldn't tolerate it, of course. Couldn't tolerate its faults. Everything in our house had to be perfect. Had to be as flawless as Mother. That sickening creature! So cruel and so certain of her own perfection!"

Mother picks up a stick off the ground. I know she misses her dog, she's missing it right now. What did they do to Mother's dog? What could they do to it, even if it wasn't perfect?

"They made it seem like an accident. They deliberately shattered a pane of glass and they deliberately scattered the pieces in the garden. They knew how overexcited he was, that he'd run around and cut himself. Or maybe the driver did it with his own hands."

Mother isn't able to speak. She's clenched her hands into fists. Mother doesn't speak when that happens. She can't.

Mother has a nightmare about a white dog with a cut throat.

That's what they've done to my mother. They cut her dog's throat with a piece of glass!

An accident! Mother, how could they do that to you?

"Come on, Bambi, let's get out of here."

First Mother walks over to the hornbeam tree, alone. She bends over to stroke the slab of stone on the ground, the tombstone she put there for her dog. She strokes the stone for a long time, like it's her dog's head.

Mother's saying good-bye to her dog. She won't tell me its name. If I know its name, the sorrow will spread. With its name, the sorrow spreads more; that's what she says.

"Let's run away, Bambi."

Holding hands, Mother and I begin running; we're out of the Vacant Lot in no time, at the end of the road now, speeding over the cobblestones, skipping steps as we race down to the main street.

There, the Bosphorus meets us. The same Bosphorus we saw just a little while earlier, from the torn box front of the Vacant Lot, but now it's right in front of us, flowing clean and strong.

"Let's leave this place immediately," Mother says. "Let's run away before bad memories pull us down to the bottom."

We jump into a taxi.

"Eminönü," Mother tells the driver. "A place where Mother never set foot."

"Excuse me?" says the driver.

"That second bit wasn't meant for you. Take us to Eminönü, please.

"My mother would go only to certain areas of Istanbul, to neighborhoods that wouldn't compromise her dignity, her perfection. She truly considered herself to be some kind of sultana or princess, that icy witch."

Grandmother, she's dead now, gone. She's not here anymore, in this city, or in this world.

"There's a dream I've never told you about," Mother says. "A nightmare that always ties me up in knots. Mother hasn't died. She's alive. I thought she was dead, but I only imagined it so I could bear living. She's alive and she's watching me. She's having me watched and followed so that just at the moment when I truly believe I'm rid of her, she can spring out and say, 'I'm still alive.' Choking me to death at the horror of that moment. Destroying me."

"But Grandmother's dead, Mom. I'm sure of it. She's not alive and she's not having you watched. She can't have you or anyone followed. I'm sure of it."

"I'm sure of it too, when I'm not having nightmares. Otherwise, we wouldn't have eaten up all her money, Bambi. Believe me, if she were around, we wouldn't have spent a cent. We wouldn't have been able to sell any of her properties. That's how I know she's dead. We've been gnawing away at her fortune for years now."

"What about your father, Mom? He's been dead a long time too, hasn't he?"

Mother's eyes are on something beyond the window of the taxi. She's devouring Istanbul with her eyes. This city isn't doing Mother any good.

I don't ask any more questions. I rest my head on Mother's knees and nod off.

This city has ground Mother down, and I don't like it, not at all.

And I never will.

BEAUTIFUL PRISON

"HERE COMES THE third Coconut Man!"

I slip through the waves and run toward Mother.

Mother's lying on a chaise longue in the shade of a palm tree, reading a book.

Those were the days we often went to Thailand in the wintertime. After a couple of nights in Bangkok, we'd go directly to the islands and to the beach. Without delay, we'd go mostly to Koh Samet.

We love several of the beaches on the island, but there's one in particular, a tiny one. Our Secret Beach, Mother calls it.

There are only two rooms at the end of the beach, at the very top where the sand meets the rocky cliffs. There are two beautifully decorated rooms. Mother takes them both.

I make pictures with my pastel paints in one of the two rooms so I'm not lonely. I spread them all out on the floor, and sometimes I fall asleep when I get up onto the bed to look at them. The sunlight dribbles through the curtains and dances on top of me.

Mother comes and wakes me with a kiss. We gather up my pictures and return to our room with our favorites.

"Come on, Bambi," Mother says, "back to our real room."

When we step out into the garden stretching before us, I do cartwheels across the grass. I somersault. Mother's thrilled. She was never able to do cartwheels, one after another, when she was little. "It might have something to do with how happy you are, Bambi. I'd tip over before I managed even two in a row."

It's like an unexpected pillow placed high up on the rocks: our soft, green garden. It looks out over the ocean. I mean, *we* look out. Evenings, swaying in our hammocks, we watch the waves and the rocks and the endlessness of the ocean. And as the sun slips away, Mother and I wave good-bye. It slips away so nice and slow.

At night, up on the rocks in our unexpected garden, the moon wheels for us alone. Amid the stars, scattered and strewn. "It's a secret system," says Mother, "and the garden closest to the stars is ours. We don't have to share it with anyone, it's our garden with a view, Bambi; it's only for us. If we heard them, the others, its beauty would be marred."

Mornings we skip down from the cliff to the chaise lounges on the sand, to be right on the ocean.

"It's wonderful here, Mom," I say, running toward the waves. I can't stay away from the ocean and its dizzying waves.

We buy flippers and a mask at one of the markets on the big beach. I search the ocean floor for cockles. Most of the ones I find are full, and I toss them back into the sea.

We're constantly gathering pebbles, pieces of coral, and cockles. Our room's overflowing with them. The empty room next door is also filling up with tiny stones and shells. It's not lonely anymore.

Coconut Men come and go. Sometimes we get the little ones, sometimes the big ones.

The little coconuts are soft inside, with only a little juice. The man gives us spoons, and we scrape at the flesh inside until we've eaten it up. The big ones are full of juice, but they're hard inside, and we chew and chew the pieces we break off. We've created a coconut corner in our garden, where we line the shells up in a row.

Then there's the Fruit and Nut Man, carrying around an ice chest of ingredients for mango salad. The mangoes are sliced into strips and presented on a plastic plate. He sprinkles hot spices and chopped nuts on top. I love spicy mango salad, the way it burns my lips when I eat it.

And I love to watch the Pareu Man pulling out his brightly printed cloths. Boredom's impossible on this beach; there's too much to do.

But my favorite thing of all is to go to the big beach around the bend and sprawl out on the sand with Mother where the sea meets it, or at least retreats almost all the way.

The ocean is reluctant to retreat from the sand. It keeps crashing back, pounding us, trying to suck us in and swallow us up.

"Just look at it, frothing up into a rage because it can't swallow us," says Mother. "Hold tight, Bambi. No one can catch us, even the ocean." Mother and I hold hands. The ocean grabs at our legs and tries to drag us away. But it can't. All it can do is splash and pound, making us laugh. Finally it goes away.

Most of the time, we eat at the restaurant up on the rocks where we're staying. The waitress is sweet and the food is good. She's teaching us how to say "hello" in Thai, and "how are you" and "thank you."

Mother gets fed up with her sweetness. "That's the candy-coated people of Thailand for you," she says, taking her eyes off the girl. "Some of them are like her: sweeter than sweet. And then there are the ones who are snakier than actual snakes. There are Candy Girls and Dragon Ladies and nothing in between."

"Mom, we're so happy here. No one could ever find us. Can't we stay here like this forever?"

"Believe me, it won't be long before we're bursting with boredom, exploded to pieces," says Mother. "Don't you see it's a beautiful prison? We'll get soft here. I'll forget everything, be unable to sense danger. And as for them, they'll waste no time. It'll become easy to track us down and trap us. I'm happy for now, Bambi. But when the time comes, we have to be able to leave this place too."

And the time does come. The day we have to leave Koh Samet.

As we gather up our things, the Dragon Lady who owns our rooms appears in the doorway and says in broken English, "So much coral you got. You can't take off island. Is illegal, you know?"

"We didn't get the coral from the sea," Mother explains. "These are all pieces we found on the beach."

"Police throw you in prison later," Dragon Lady insists. When she says "prison," she clamps her wrists together, as though handcuffed, and raises her arms in the direction of our faces.

"Don't be ridiculous." Mother's voice is climbing. "My daughter's only taking two or three pieces that washed up on the beach, as a keepsake."

But Dragon Lady doesn't know enough English to understand her. "Police take you to prison!" She thrusts her "handcuffed" hands into our faces. Again.

"She might go and inform the police. To get her cut of the bribe they'll extort. Or simply to practice this week's obligatory act of wickedness. One mustn't get rusty." Mother orders the woman out of our room. Out of our room and out of our memories of the wonderful days we spent on this island. Out. Out.

Dragon Lady leaves at last.

"Behind the smiles and the sweetness, the easygoing nature, and their oh-so-sublime Buddhist beliefs are the cruelest prisons, the harshest tortures; they're a people capable of the worst atrocities," Mother says. "It's the duplicity I can't bear. I prefer my poison presented in a bowl, as poison. Not as melted sugar meant to fool a child."

Mother can't bear the word "police" under any circumstances.

"She's spoiled everything, Bambi. Let's not wait until morning. Let's get out of here right now."

We cram a few more things into our knapsacks and rush down to the big beach to catch the last motorboat off the island.

"I'm certain Dragon Lady will return all of our pebbles to the beach." Mother now smiles, on the boat. "We didn't even have to compensate her for her services."

On the huge bed in one of the rooms, Mother and I lined up pebbles, pieces of coral, and cockleshells to spell out "FUCKING."

And on the bed in the other room: "BITCH!"

"We told her what she was," Mother says, her eyes scanning the sea. "Of course, just like all the other rude souls, she'll never attain a level of awareness. But if nothing else, we left letting her know exactly what she is."

"We spelled it out well, Mother," I say, resting my head on her breast. I'm filled with sea smell and Mother Scent. I could burst from happiness.

"It was a work of art, Bambi," Mother says. "But you're my one and only masterpiece."

Mother and I were so happy on that island. Even Dragon Lady couldn't take that away from us. And the message in pebbles was wonderful.

You were wonderful, Mother. The days we spent together were wonderful. Until they caught up to us, no one could possibly imagine just how happy we were.

HOSTAGE

WE WENT TO that country only once, to Tunisia.

"What a démodé hotel," Mother says upon our arrival. "Just look at it, everything left over from the sixties. That's what makes it so nice and peaceful."

I'm still little. As little as Mother wishes me to be.

Mother will imagine for many years that I don't know what happened in Tunisia, that I can't remember anything. And I'll pretend too. That I don't remember much at all, can't remember a thing. Not a thing, almost.

When Mother lists the countries we've visited, she never mentions Tunisia. She'll make it seem we never went there; and she'll make certain I don't remember either.

That's what I'll do.

For a long time, I won't remember Tunisia. I won't think about it at all. But then, one day, years later, because of a color, the color orange—yes, I see a plastic plate the color orange—it all comes swarming into my consciousness. Crystal clear. Frame by frame. Scene by scene. Black and white, all of it. Except for the orange plate.

Mother and I are in Tunisia. I'm still little. Still little enough to sit on her lap on a canvas chaise longue with a wooden frame. Still little enough to carry around coloring books. I color in pictures all day long.

"You're completely wrapped up in those pictures of yours," Mother laughs. "You never even look up."

My hair was a much lighter shade of blond then, in ringlets. Like a doll.

I raise my head and smile at Mother. "You color in Snow White's dress, Mommy! But make it stripes, all stripes."

"All right, baby," says Mother.

Mother's great at coloring. She finds amazing designs for all the stupid, boring clothing. She draws stripes, stars, circles, and funny shapes. Then she carefully colors them in with the pencils. Each one of them is different. Each of them is sewn out of the funniest, most beautiful cloth in the world.

As we sit at our table on the sand with our colored pencils, I see that all of the life and joy is draining away from Mother's face. I sense it, even at that age.

"What is it? What happened, Mommy?"

"It's nothing, baby. Keep doing your pictures. I'll go up to our room and get your bucket and beach toys."

"I don't want them!"

Mother begins running toward our room. I watch her race off, puzzled. Mother never runs away, leaving me behind. What happened?

Two old ladies are slowly walking toward the empty table next to ours. One of them holds the other by the arm. They creep along. Like a pair of sand crabs. Filled with curiosity, I watch.

I'm not sure how I feel about them, but as I watch them approach from far off, I sense that they are what made Mother run away.

The old lady with the snow-white hair has unseeing eyes. That's why the younger one has taken her arm. That's why the old lady holds her head high, smiling into a distance she can't see.

I stare at the blind old woman, spellbound. She looks like the grannies in fairy tales: hair gathered into a bun, a black silk dress with a white collar, an ivory brooch, everything about her. Like the grannies in stories, the ones who seem good-hearted, but aren't. They're both like that.

"That woman, the one who just went running off, isn't that her daughter?" asks Blind Old Woman. "That murdered woman's daughter?"

"Shhh," hisses the Other Woman. "There's a little girl at the table, listening."

"It's her daughter," says the first one. "She was pregnant when her mother was killed. As far as I know, no one's seen her face since then. If you ask me, she's running away. Somehow she was mixed up in all that."

They're speaking Turkish. Our language. And they're talking about Mother. They know my mother and they're talking about her. Badly.

But no one knows us. No one ever talks about Mother. I know that something terribly strange and terribly wrong is happening, I feel it deep inside. I begin crying over my coloring books.

"See, the girl's crying," says the Other Woman. "She heard you. I've asked you repeatedly to keep your voice down, haven't I? And how do you know it's the daughter, how'd you recognize her? Perhaps it wasn't her. Maybe it's someone similar, that's all. How could you possibly recognize any of them after all this time?"

"The smell," says Blind Old Woman. "The smell of the past and the smell of fear." She recognizes the need to lower her voice. But it's such a high-pitched, childlike quaver that I'm able to hear every word.

Each word pierces my heart with a force I can't understand. I'm trembling and in tears.

"Get the girl and bring her over to our table."

The Other Woman plants herself right next to me, with a deeply unsettling smile. A wound of a smile. Her eyes are blue, almost blindingly blue. She strokes my hair as she speaks. I'm scared of her. Her teeth are tiny and white, they're like baby teeth. Her old face and baby teeth are hideous.

"We're Turkish too, my child. You're Turkish, aren't you? That auntie over there recognized your mother. We used to be your grandmother's neighbors."

Over at the next table, Blind Woman nods and smiles as she fixes her unseeing eyes onto me. With a thin, white, wrinkled hand, she gestures for me to go to her. "Come over and join us, you beautiful girl."

"Mommy! Mommy!" I'm still in my seat, racked with sobs.

We've fallen on people we should never have. We've seen people we should never have seen. We're in terrible trouble. I feel it with all my heart. Please, Mommy, come rescue me.

The Other Woman begins to caress me. "Don't cry, little girl. We know who you are. We love you. Aren't you the sweetest little thing. Come on, I'll get you an ice cream. Sister, just look at her!"

Icy, bony hands seize me and lift me from the chair. I'm forced into her embrace and carried to the other table. I'm shrinking, smaller and smaller, anxious, terrified. Mommy, I'm scared. Come quick, save me!

I didn't know how much time passed. Like in a nightmare. Either a very long time or a very short one. I sit at their table, cowering, trying to swallow my hiccups. The tears I can't stop trickling down my cheeks. In front of me, on a huge plate, is a pile of ice cream.

A huge orange plastic plate. The scoops are brown and white. Chocolate and vanilla. The Other Woman is forcing a spoonful of ice cream into my mouth.

"Come on, eat up, look how nice it is. Delicious ice cream made from goat's milk. Eat it up, you pretty little thing. My sister got it just for you."

Blind Woman reaches out a hand and squeezes my shoulder. "Why do you keep crying? Eat your ice cream. Look, your mother's nowhere to be seen. Maybe you'll be our little girl now. All ours, and we'll go everywhere together. What do you say to that, sister?"

They laugh. Looking at each other, not looking at each other, touching hands, in high spirits. My tears apparently please them; they're laughing and having fun. They're going to kidnap me! Mommy, where are you? Come save me. The wicked grannies are going to steal me from you.

I can't hold it in anymore; it flows warm from between my legs across the white chair. They mustn't see. They mustn't see me wet myself. Or they'll throw me into an oven. Mother will never be able to find me then. They'll burn me alive. They'll do away with me before Mommy can rescue me.

A young waiter comes up to the table and whispers something into the ear of the Other Woman. She springs up from the table, begins running toward the garden in front of the hotel as fast as she can.

"Where are you going?" Blind Woman shouts, cutting short her fun. "Did she send for you? Don't you dare go! Don't you know who she is?"

She seizes my hand. "See, I've taken you hostage. If that killer mother of yours does anything to my sister, I've got you hostage. If she harms a hair on my sister's head, she'll get what's coming to her!"

Gathering all my strength, I break free of her hand. I'm off the chair, running.

"Help! Save my sister, quick! She's killing my sister! She's killing her in the garden!" Blind Woman shouts in that terrible, little-girl voice.

Mother clasps me as I run through the garden. She picks me up and smothers me with kisses. "Baby, forget everything. Nothing happened. Wipe everything from your mind. We never came here. It's erased. It's all gone now. Poof! See, all gone, all you saw and heard. Vanished!"

But years later at the sight of an orange plastic plate, I remember everything again. Like pressing an orange rewind button. I'm grown now. I don't tell Mother.

I don't tell her what I remember. What's the need?

THE SECRETARY

I HAVE TO say it, he wasn't very nice.

He was a bad guy. Bad as they come.

And forever contradicting himself! He'd start out saying something and contradict himself before he even got to the end of the sentence. All empty words and hot air. "Boss's bull" is what we called it, his lies and bluster. Of course, it's not like he had to answer to us. We'd sit and listen to him, because we had to.

Always talking out of the side of his mouth!

He'd twist and turn everything he said, and in the end, he'd get whatever he wanted. Whatever was best for him. He'd make sure of it.

The hours we worked, the terms and conditions, our salaries: he'd beat us down with his tongue until we gave in. And that was that. Whatever he said, that was it.

And when the dust settled, everything always turned out best for him. And worse for you. I mean, for everyone working here at the hotel.

He irritated the hell out of us all. The way he put people down, always managing to find their weak spots, jabbing with his tongue.

We all worked for him. What could we do? What was the point?

He came from somewhere far away, and he rose higher and higher. Until he owned a hotel. And then a chain of hotels. That's the way they wrote it up in the newspapers: a success story, they said.

People looking in from the outside liked him a lot. A straight-talking man of his word, that's what they thought! Self-made, successful, and all that! It's enough to drive you crazy. If you want the real story, ask us.

Only when you've been working for him for years do you get it. When you're worn out and fed up. We always made fun of him behind his back. With jokes and gestures. But always behind his back. We were afraid of losing our jobs, of course.

He'd fire anyone at the drop of a hat. One day you're his best friend, his right-hand man, and then the next thing you know you're out the door! Cry all you want, he couldn't care less. That's the kind of guy he was. Dozens of people working for him, and not one of them liked him, not a single one.

Some talked back when he cheated them. They'd get a warning, that's all, for what it's worth. He always won out in the end.

I don't know why he fought with that woman, I haven't got any idea what went on between them. She was a hotel guest, he was the hotel manager. None of us are even sure if they'd met before that day.

The guys used to talk about that woman and her daughter all the time.

Especially the daughter. A real beauty, they said, sweet as can be. As far as I understood, she was still pretty young, just a kid, really. Around thirteen or fourteen.

But she was still a kid, so it's not like they were trying to flirt with her or anything; not that their mouths were watering, not really. But I have to say, they did go on about her: her hair, her eyes, her legs, her ass!

I saw her a couple of times, in the distance, they pointed her out to me. Sure, she was a pretty enough kid. But her mother, the clothes. It wasn't normal. We don't get any guests like that here at our hotel.

They weren't like Turks, but they weren't like Germans either, or Russians. You couldn't tell where they came from; it was like they were from another world.

They were all alone, and they were here for a long time. In the off-season, when no one swims in the sea. The weather getting colder by the day, the sun gone. But still they stayed on at the hotel, for the longest time. If they hadn't stayed for so long, maybe no one would have noticed them.

I wasn't the first person to enter my boss's office. No. My best friend went in to get a signature or something. Did she ever scream!

Never in my life have I heard anyone scream like that.

Maybe that's why I froze when I went in after her. I just stood there and stared. Of course, I'd never seen anyone with a cut throat before. I stood there and stared until the office filled up with people.

She'd used the letter opener there on the desk to do it, to cut his throat. An expert incision to the jugular, that's what the police said later. His head was thrown back; he had such a comfortable office chair, if you didn't see his throat, you'd think he was having a snooze. You'd think he was finally getting a moment of rest from all his lying and cheating. If you looked only at his face—not his neck, of course—he seemed peaceful as can be.

His body was sitting slumped in that chair like he was asleep.

That woman must have used the letter opener on his desk. She put it right back when she was done. That's what she always did, or so the papers say. She used whatever she could get her hands on.

Bottles, switchblades, ashtrays, jackknives. I suppose she got really mad and just blew her top. At something they did or said. So then she looked around, and grabbed the first thing that came to her hand. It's not that she always carried something with her, to kill.

She just lost it. That's what they all said about her, what they wrote in the papers. Our boss was involved, so, as you can imagine, we read all the papers and talked about it for days.

Funny I put it that way, isn't it? That he was "involved." Was I upset or even surprised?

Of course I was upset and surprised.

I mean, I had no idea so much blood could come out of one person, that people even have that much blood in them.

The whole front of him, his lap and legs!

And the front of his desk!

Blood spurting everywhere. And he was a little guy, he couldn't have been more than five-and-a-half feet or so. Tall or not, he had an awful lot of blood inside him, enough to run down the chair and soak the silk carpet on the floor, soak everything in blood.

And it's not as if she was working for him. I mean, as far as I can tell, that woman didn't have a reason to kill him.

She was just a guest here! She could have packed up and gone any time. So why'd she kill him? Why get yourself into trouble like that?

And it wasn't the first time. What a terrible temper she must have had. A real hothead. I suppose she just snapped.

Something to do with her daughter is what we thought. That's got to be it. Did someone say something to her? Do something to her? No one could think of anything; we talked about it, but we couldn't come up with a thing.

So who picked the fight, and why? They were guests. And he was the boss.

But he never could keep his mouth shut. No, he always had a cutting word for everyone, he did. King of the hill he was, at least here at the hotel. The way he'd strut around the place, a regular rooster.

He had it coming!

What am I saying? That's not what I meant. It's terrible what happened to him. I mean, he was my boss. And he's been paying my salary all these years.

Not that he didn't make me pay through the nose for every cent! Oh, he made sure of that.

As though beating down his employees was a personal pleasure. I've never seen anyone like him in my life; that's how bad he was. And I hope I never meet anyone else like him. Or have to work for a rat like him ever again.

How come he didn't scream? We didn't hear a thing!

His throat must have been sliced just like that, bam. As he sat in his room on his throne.

They were so sure of themselves!

They even checked out. The girl did, I mean. While the mother was packing up their things. Taking a shower, changing her clothes.

They left a lot behind, though. Clothes, drapes, branches, stones, all kinds of stuff.

Their room was full of stuff when they cleared out. They just grabbed what they could carry and hailed a taxi to the airport.

But that's what they always did. They had to be able to run off, just like that, with a couple of small bags.

Am I upset? Yeah, I am. In the end, someone died. But if you were to ask me whose dead body I'd most like to see, I'd have to say my boss's. That's the truth of the matter. All that blood, running everywhere. But I can't say I'm angry with the woman who did it. It's like she's getting even for all the years of whatever it is they've been doing to her, out for revenge.

I wouldn't have been surprised if anyone at the hotel had done it. It all comes down to kismet, I suppose, and she was the one. The mother of that beautiful girl.

What else can you say?

THE OFFICIAL MERCEDES

I'M STILL LITTLE.

But not that little. Not too little to remember everything, in detail.

It was during the time when we spent weeks, months, in London. During that time, we'd visit toy stores every day and carry armloads of toys back to our room.

"Look how wide the sidewalks are in this city," Mother says. "Wide enough to get around easily with a baby. But the Tube's still impossible. You'd need two people to get a stroller up and down all those stairs. A woman and a baby alone could never do it. That's how they expect us to live our lives, Bambi. But I've been able to raise you on my own. I've managed their stairs and their sidewalks and their revolving doors on my own. Because the joy you've brought me has made me strong."

Mother and I are holding hands as we walk to the Peter Pan statue in the park.

The birds are full of life today. And so are you.

We've slipped free of the days when we couldn't leave our hotel room. Watching television under the covers all day long. Staying in our room for weeks on end. Locked in.

We watched as alcoholic housewives said that they were alcoholics because of their mothers, watched as they blubbered and shrieked.

We watched as men fought with women who had run off with their best friends who fought with women. The best friends fought with other women, hurling insults and making obscene gestures.

We watched as girls addicted to drugs blamed their mothers and fathers, and watched as their mothers and fathers cried and carried on, and it always ended in tearful hugs.

We sat inside all day long watching the worst television had to offer.

"Their banalities disgust me. They force me to remember that we share the same planet, and they turn me to stone inside," you repeated, again and again.

"What a terrible place. A stomping ground of depravity.

"They are many, and bad. We're all alone, Bambi," you said.

You said many things about how they made you feel inside. But you continued to watch them, Mother. Because you had nothing better in Those Moments. That's what you said.

And then Those Moments were gone, out of our life.

There's an unexpected entrance to Hyde Park right across from our hotel.

We enter and walk for a long time. We visit that wonderful statue of Peter Pan in Kensington Gardens.

We rub our hands against his shoes. Then we rub our hands together and make a wish. We don't tell each other what our wishes are so they won't fly away and vanish. Hidden wishes come true. Because Peter Pan is good luck. Lucky and magical, as is his statue. A wishing statue.

We go to toy stores. We go to bookstores. Then back to toy stores. And to bookstores again.

We're away from that enormous bed that fills our room, the sickening blankets, the television directly in front of us, against the window.

I'm happy, Mother. We walk the streets of London, all day. You tell me about the new strollers, how much better designed they are now. You tell me how you tried three different models and how difficult it was until I started walking. Even in London.

"Thank goodness you started walking at ten months, baby. I think you couldn't bear how difficult it was for me, so you learned to walk as soon as you could. You're my baby, perfect, and you couldn't bear to see your mommy struggling."

No mother could ever love her child as much as you love me, Mother. Not that I know any other mothers or children. But I do know about them from films and books. And I know about my grandmother, who was even less of a mother than a Mother Crow.

But I'm certain, Mother. No other mothers love their children enough to bring them up all on their own. But you did. You can do anything, Mother. Anything.

We're at the biggest of the toy stores that day. "When I was a girl, this was the most prestigious toy store in the city. Prestigious enough for your grandmother to select a doll for her daughter.

"Your grandmother never let me have the dolls I wanted. Only the ones she chose. The most expensive, elaborate ones. And the coldest.

"She'd always pick out the most soulless one for me. Little ice queens that reminded me of her."

We decide to look at model cars too. Even though neither of us likes toy cars made of metal. Our favorites are the huge stuffed animals and dolls with funny faces. That's what we always get.

In a display case in the middle of the shop are some metal cars made in Germany. Exact replicas of famous makes and models. The doors open, and so do the hoods. Everything's perfect: the mirrors, windows, windshield wipers.

"Ass cars for assholes," Mother says. Then she presses two fingers against her lips.

Like she always does after a curse she doesn't want me to hear.

We both laugh. Mother's so happy and so much fun. No one has a mother like my mother. I'm certain of that.

We stand in front of a black Mercedes for the longest time. "Look, it's your grandfather's official Mercedes, same year, same model. I hate people who drive a Mercedes. They remind me of my father. And of the worldwide sovereignty of arrogant tyrants."

Mother's rooted to the spot in front of the Mercedes.

"Mother, are you OK? Mother, let's leave this place. Are you all right, Mom?"

"Just a minute, Bambi." She's trying to come back up from the depths. She's trying to return to my side. I know that.

She calls over a salesclerk. The display window is opened. It's wrapped and put in a bag. We've bought the Official Mercedes.

The moment we get out onto the street, she tears open the box, she dashes the Mercedes against the sidewalk. The Mercedes is fine. It's sturdy because it's made in Germany.

Mother picks it up. "Come on, Bambi, run with me."

There's a luxurious department store where my grandmother would shop for clothes. Sometimes Mother and I have lunch in the cafeteria there, then we have fun looking at all the ugly things they sell.

We run into that store and up to the top floor. Mother's going to throw the Mercedes off of the balcony of the cafeteria. I'm certain of it.

"No, Mommy. No. No! It might hit someone in the head, a child."

"I'll be careful, Bambi."

"No, Mommy. Please don't. Please, Mommy."

Mother catches me by the hand and shakes me. "Your mother would never hurt anyone who didn't deserve it. Trust me, Bambi."

She throws the Mercedes out onto the street. The Mercedes is twisted and bent. But it's still a Mercedes. A wondrous German import.

By the time we reach the street, several cars have driven over it. Mother leaves me on the sidewalk and goes into the street to get it. It's fit for the scrap heap but still determined to preserve its status as a Mercedes.

Later, in the bathroom, we douse it with rubbing alcohol and set it on fire. It's scorched now, but persists in being a Mercedes. That night we put it into a bag and carry it to the Peter Pan statue.

"We'll bury what's left of it," Mother says. "We'll bury this car the same way we buried your grandfather's evil, that's all we want. Isn't that right, Bambi?"

"Yes, Mother."

"We want him buried and gone from our memories, the same way we want his official Mercedes buried and gone."

"First we wrecked it. Then we burned it, Mother."

"So be it, Bambi. You can't possibly grasp the long reach of tyrants, the range of their evil. And you never will."

We bury the toy Mercedes between two trees over by the Peter Pan statue, and we stamp on the ground above it. Mother wants me to remember the exact spot it's buried.

"We'll stamp our feet on it every time we come here; and, if no one's around, we'll pee on it."

I know she's joking. The birds in her voice are saying this. Yes, they are birds of prey. But they'd never tear at anyone's heart.

THE HORRIBLE COUPLE

MOTHER AND I are at a winter resort.

I'm taking ski lessons a few hours a day, from a dim instructor who thinks he's handsome and witty.

"It's not as important as swimming, of course," Mother says, "but being a good skier could be useful too, baby. They're all survival skills."

When I was smaller we used to winter in some of these ski resorts. I was a good skier back then.

"She's like a snow bunny," Mother said, "the way my baby glides along, at one with the snow."

My body hasn't forgotten how to ski; it's taken just a few days for it to come back. I'm turning into a snow bunny again, Mother. But she won't let me ski without the instructor, so I'm condemned to his idiotic jokes and his running mouth.

"It would make me too anxious, Bambi. I can't be expected to wait in our room, worrying about you the entire time. Idiot or not, you need someone with you while you're skiing."

Mother reads and smokes in our room. She looks out at the slopes from the window and smokes. She's smoking more than ever now. When she wakes up in the morning, she coughs for hours.

"Surely I'm entitled to this one small comfort, Bambi. I need the damn things. And I never smoke when you're in the room. I can control myself if I have to."

The only time Mother comes down out of our room is when I swim in the hotel pool. Sometimes she times me on a stopwatch, jotting down my times in a black notebook.

"A world champion! My very own secret world champion. I don't think there's anyone your age that could swim fifty meters that fast."

Sometimes we have dinner in the ski resort's restaurant, always before anyone comes down, or after they're all gone. At other times I prepare a tray and bring it up to the room. Mother isn't eating much these days. She doesn't feel like it. She's fed up with food and everything else.

There are times when Mother seems to be on the verge of one of Those Moments. It brings my heart to my mouth to see her about to succumb to them. But so far she's been managing to slip free, just in time.

"I've slipped free this time too, Bambi. I'm not bad at all. In fact, by my own standards, I'm doing quite well."

She starts laughing at the word "standards." Then she gasps. And coughs and coughs. Mother's body can't tolerate this intimacy with cigarettes any longer.

One day the ski resort fills up completely. It's not the usual influx of the weekend crowd, it's the midterm break. The hotel fills with children, parents, nannies; suddenly it's so full we can't breathe.

I see that Mother can't breathe in this crowd. She grows visibly weaker by the day, her strength melting away. I can see it.

"Once I pull myself together, we'll get out of here. They've left me gasping for air. How was I to know about the midterm break?"

A young woman is supervising her two little skinny-legged, curly-haired, unlovable sons as they splash about in the pool. She looks like the women in those silly films: her short hair dyed blond, upturned nose, enormous brown eyes.

"Creature of Hollywood!" Mother says. "Overly sweet, overly chatty, overly clubby. Dreadful! I wonder if she deliberately waits for you to come down to the pool. The more I try to avoid her, the more often I run into her!"

She tries to exchange greetings with Mother. She tries to talk to me, calling me "that pretty girl," and Mother is about to lose it; I can see that.

"Oh, look! If it isn't that pretty girl here at the pool again. Her mother sure makes her work hard, doesn't she?"

Her voice is a little bell; her inquisitive eyes—already enormous, now widened into saucers—are staring at Mother.

"ShirleyTempleMegRyan is assailing us with her sweetness again," Mother says. "Drowning us in her syrupy sense of self-worth. Do we really have to endure these cutesy attacks?"

Every time we go down to the pool, I'm terrified she'll be there. The more she sticks to us, the more she irritates Mother. And the more she irritates Mother, the more relentless she becomes, popping out at us everywhere we go.

Sometimes she and her sons corner me on the ski slope. She makes a point of mentioning Mother. She must be thirsting to fill us with more disgust. I can't believe that she won't back off.

One day she suddenly appears as we're getting our key from reception. "That pretty girl's mother must have forgotten the sunscreen. Look at the poor thing's little nose and cheeks, bright red!"

"You don't say," says Mother, her voice in shards. "I guess this pretty girl's mother is always neglecting her."

There's no way she doesn't realize how much she's upsetting Mother. And me. She must see—or at least sense—how tense that makes me. It's impossible that she doesn't. So why won't she leave us alone?

"Ah, the pretty girl's mother finally speaks," she tinkles, clapping her hands. Flush with victory, her voice tinkles and chimes.

"Now that you've won, you might get off our backs," says Mother.

"What's that supposed to mean? I'm just trying to be nice to your daughter, and to you. You seem so unusual, so different from everyone else." For the first time, I can hear the tinkle has become muted.

"Is it possible that you're completely unaware how profoundly your presence disturbs us?"

"Well, I never! How rude! No one talks to me like that. What did I do to you? I was only trying to be friends." She starts to cry, suddenly a little girl. She's all sobs and shaking shoulders.

"You're impossible," Mother says. "You've made it impossible for us. You're a truly horrible person."

"Horrible? You're calling me horrible?" She's sobbing even louder now, the loudest I've ever heard!

"Honey, what happened? What have they done to you?" A horrible man lunges at us. He has a pair of spinning, beady eyes that look like buttons tacked on above his big mouth and nose; a phony through and through. His teeth are too white, too fake. A

Phony Man, standing there in a showy snowsuit straight out of a shop window.

"They in-insulted me. I was just t-trying to be nice to them, because they were alone. I felt sorry for them. You know me, honey."

"I know you. You're a sociopath," says Mother. "A compulsive liar, and you have an utter disregard for boundaries."

"Who are you to talk to my wife like that!" Phony Man bellows.

They're pressing in on us: the doormen, the floor attendants, the secretaries dying of boredom in the office only moments before, the unlovable sons and their Filipino nannies, all swarming around us.

"Just who do you think you are? Do you know who I am? How dare you talk to my children's mother like that!"

Mother's overwhelmed. Phony Man raises his arm, making it appear that he's barely able to contain himself, that he might beat my mother at any moment.

"Sir, please, sir!" says the crowd. Voices intervene with, "You're right, of course, but she is a woman, after all."

"I know exactly who and what you are," hisses Mother. "But you're too much of an idiot even to know yourself."

"Let me at her, let me at her!" yells Phony Man.

"Honey, honey. She's crazy. Please don't, honey," shrieks ShirleyTempleMegRyan, clinging to her husband even more tightly.

Mother squeezes my hand as she looks me directly in the eye. "I'm going up to our room. Ask them for our bill, and have them call a taxi, Bambi. Quick."

"OK, Mother," I say, staring at this Horrible Couple full of hatred. If I got my hands on a knife at that moment, I'd stab those two a hundred times, a thousand times. I could sever their necks clean, like a couple of sick chickens.

For their shameful theatrics, for upsetting Mother and me, and for blaming us: I could kill them both.

I could kill them without blinking.

THE WINDY PLACE

THE WIND'S BLOWING, hard.

It's sunny; a winter sun. We wake up to a bright winter sun every day. But it's very windy. The wind's noisy; it whistles.

The wind keeps Mother awake. She says the whistling keeps her from settling down inside.

"My soul's on a thorn, Bambi. They might be nearby. They might have found our tracks. It doesn't bode well for the wind to be this loud. And actually, it's a nice wind. I wish it didn't make me feel so bad inside."

"Get on your Sea Bed, Mommy. Let the waves rock you to sleep."

Mother taught me about the Sea Bed. When I'm upset—I mean, when I feel bad because Mother's upset—when Mother senses they could be nearby, if we're afraid of getting caught, or if we're troubled, uneasy, for any reason, the Sea Bed calms me down and puts me to sleep, just like Mother taught me.

Picture yourself on an inflatable bed on a calm sea. Tell yourself to feel it, tell your inner self. Gently and slowly, while lying in bed on your back. The next thing you know, you're on your back on a Sea Bed.

"Let life gently rock you from below, like the ocean. You're on a Sea Bed. Rocking, side to side. It doesn't matter where it takes you. Let time flow. Let yourself flow. Further and further from the bad times, on the Sea Bed. Swaying, calmer and calmer, drifting away."

I'm still young. But I'm not that young anymore. I can't be.

No matter what I wear, how my hair is done up, the baby colors chosen by my mother, I can't be that young, not as young as she wants. Not anymore.

Bambi tried to think. But the savage noises grew louder and louder and paralyzed Bambi's senses. He heard nothing but those noises. They numbed him while amidst the howling, shouting and crashing he could hear his own heart pounding. He felt nothing but curiosity and did not realize he was trembling in every limb. From time to time his mother whispered in his ear, "Stay close to me." She was shouting, but in the uproar it sounded to Bambi as if she were whispering. Her "Stay close to me" encouraged him. It was like a chain holding him. Without it he would have rushed off senselessly, and he heard it at the very moment when his wits were wandering and he wanted to dash away.

He looked around. All sorts of creatures were swarming past, scampering blindly over one another. A pair of weasels ran by like thin snake-like streaks. The eye could scarcely follow them.

Mother's scratchy voice is dividing our room into squares. The room, full of lines, side to side, top to bottom, is divided by her voice. The lines intersect, becoming squares.

"I know all of *Bambi* by heart, Mom. This part, and all the others."

"So you're bored with *Bambi*, are you? You've grown up, you don't want to listen."

"That's not it. It's just, I know it already."

"You're right, my Bambi." Mother pulls my head to her breast. She sniffs my hair. She kisses me. "I won't read it to you ever again."

"I've memorized it, Mom."

"That's fine, baby. Fine, you're right."

A teardrop runs out of Mother's eye. Her fingertips catch the drop sliding down her cheek. But her eyes fill up. It's there that Mother sees, as I do, that I'm growing, that I must grow. There, in that antique city, in the whistling wind, beneath a winter sun.

We're among some ruins, a fifteen-minute walk along the beach from our hotel. Mother's bought a disposable camera. We take many pictures among the columns. Of me posing among the ruins.

In fact, Mother's scared of photographs; that is to say, she's scared someone will take our picture. But she can't resist the beauty of these ruins on the seaside.

She's also frightened of me growing up. That's another reason for all the snapshots. I know that; she wants to capture me before I've grown.

I know that you want to capture me here, Mother. My growing up is as terrifying to you as the whistling wind. You're terrified. Your little girl is growing up.

"It's as though it increases the chances of us getting caught. As though the bigger you get the easier it'll be for them to find us. I can't help it, Bambi. I'm afraid of your growing up. But I'll get used to it, of course. Please, be patient with me."

I don't want to grow up either, Mother. Your fear is my fear.

You imagine you're hidden from me. That you're able to toss everything deep inside. That you're a closed box.

But we're both in that box, that same box. From now on.

If you're upset by the wind, so am I. If you can't sleep, I can: within your wakefulness is a strange sleepiness. I'm able to sleep a sleep that is half wakeful.

Right now we're among picturesque ruins at the seaside. We're staying in a hotel room, and I'm growing up. You keep snapping shots of my childhood. You want to make time stop for us, here.

I want to stop time here too.

I don't want to grow up, so you won't be frightened.

But there's no possibility of that, and we're here, facing this impossibility. Together.

The wind knows no end. You're saddened by this too. By the wind's threats. By its torments.

"It could stop, Bambi. It could quiet down, calm down. But it won't. It won't let me right myself inside. Just like your growing up won't let me. Perhaps it's crowing over the inevitability, the unavoidability of it all.

"It's whistling away, in fine fettle."

Every day Mother photographs me for hours. Sometimes as I pose, the wind blows something into my eye. Mother gets upset when we have to stop for a moment. As though terrified that the next snapshot will be of a girl suddenly grown up.

"Stand next to that column, the one back there. How did we miss a beauty like that?"

"Mother, you took a lot of photographs of that column just the other day. You've taken pictures of me next to every piece of stone in this city."

"Is that so? Like *Bambi*? Is it like memorizing *Bambi*?"

Mother throws the camera to the ground. Pieces of plastic break off.

I'm running toward Mother. She's sinking down onto the stone ruins.

Suddenly she allows herself to fall backward. Her head thuds against stone.

"Mother! Are you OK, Mom?"

I place Mother's head in my lap. The winter sun is hiding itself behind some clouds. As if even the winter sun were determined not to do us any good.

"Everything's going badly here," Mother says.

"Let's go to a sunny place, Mother. A hot place. A place away from the wind."

"The wind's busily boring it into my head: You're growing. You'll grow up."

"Mother, please don't." I start to cry. I'm afraid Mother will start beating her head on her bed of stone. The fear makes me cry. "Please, Mother. Please don't do anything bad."

Mother sits up. She pulls me toward her. "Do I frighten you so very much? Forgive me, Bambi. My beautiful girl, forgive your mother."

She springs to her feet and pulls me up to mine. We run all the way to the hotel.

Mother's conquered the wind. And suddenly my growing up no longer frightens her. Mother's pulled herself together. Never again will she read *Bambi* to me.

And now I'm growing up. I'm able to grow without upsetting Mother.

I can grow, at ease, and without upsetting Mother.

THE BUSBOY

SHE WAS GREAT. A real character and so much fun. Really.

She made you laugh; she sure made me laugh. She said things you'd never think of. Noticed things no one else would. Not hammering it home, though. And if you got it, you'd laugh. And she'd laugh with you. Like it was your reward, for understanding.

I shadowed them all the time.

I stayed near them to laugh, at a joke or something she said. To get through the day with a smile, to finish off the night right.

I was really fond of her. The mother of that pretty girl.

She was real pretty too. Real pretty to me, anyway. A tall, thin woman. And her hair was thick and black with streaks of gray, pulled right back.

Sometimes she let her hair down. She was beautiful when she did that. She was such a good person. I was forever running circles around their table, hoping they'd talk to me.

To tell you the truth, I was jealous of the girl. I'd have given anything to have a mother like that. Like her mother, I mean.

I don't care what they say about her. What do they know, anyway? They don't understand anything, so how can they understand her? They never got to know her at all. So what gives them the right to talk about her like that?

We got on so well. "Yellow Head," that's what she called me. Always smiling as she said it. She kissed me once, right on top of the head. It was all I could do not to throw my arms around her.

It was like one of those Turkish films. You know. I had to hold myself back or I'd have put my head on her breast and cried "Mother, dear Mother." Imagine how embarrassing that would have been! But now I regret it. I wish, just once, I'd told her how much I loved her, just once.

I wish I'd told her I'd never met anyone like her. That she was one of a kind. I wanted her to hear someone say what a wonderful person she was.

I couldn't care less about what happened. I wish she were my mother. I wish it so much!

Our meals are open buffet here in this holiday village. So it's collect the dirty plates, stack up some clean ones. Bring in glasses, take out the dirty ones. Sometimes she asked for red wine. Not often, every few nights. And her daughter drank beer a couple times. When she asked for wine, I'd know she was in a good mood. I'd always make sure to bring it myself.

I'd bring it over so she'd talk to me. She always had a few words, but I'd wait around to fill her glass so she'd say more. If she were my mother, that's all I'd need out of life. Of course, wanting something doesn't mean you'll get it.

They were staying in a big room. Opening up onto the garden in front. And the things they did to that room! What an amazing place they made for themselves! I stared and stared. The police had to drag me out when they arrived.

Well, the doctor's body was found in the wardrobe. He was wrapped in garbage bags so the blood wouldn't leak. And over that, layer after layer of sheets. They'd made a mummy out of him.

When the fat cleaner opened the wardrobe door, there he was. She doesn't know the word "mummy." She kept saying he looked like a "rag doll."

A big bloody rag doll!

They'd been gone for some time. When they left, the blood had probably barely seeped through the plastic and the cloth. But when they found the doctor, he was a bloody mummy.

It was all because that beautiful daughter got sick. Otherwise none of this would have happened.

She suddenly got sick. They stopped coming down to eat, going to the beach. They stayed in the room all the time.

Earlier, the girl was always swimming with her mother. Way out in the depths. Like a fish, a mermaid. She really was something of a mermaid.

And because I loved the mother, I loved the daughter too. I admit it, I was jealous, couldn't help myself. Take a look at my mother, then take a look at hers.

And how she loved her daughter. Watching her with burning eyes, troubled eyes, eyes like red-hot coals, because she loved her, a burning love. I've never seen any mother love her child that way, not even in films.

When the girl got ill, I heard about it from the other guys, that she was shaking like she had malaria. Burning up. And you can imagine how worried her mother was.

This holiday village is in the middle of nowhere. So who else do they turn to but that bastard of a doctor?

I know all about that guy, I had my own run-in with him. I cut my hand real bad in the kitchen one day and he wanted to stitch it up. Anyhow, there was this old nurse back then. "What stitches? What for?" she said. If that crazy doctor had had his way, he'd have gone at me with a needle and thread or whatever else he could get his hands on.

He was a real bastard. He'd been fired, kicked out, from other places before. From what I understand, he had a relative who helped him out. Someone got him a position here so he could laze around at the beach all day. But he was no doctor, that much was obvious.

So not only did he fail to treat the girl, he molested her or something. He does that all the time, to girls. I know everyone— the guys who work out on the beach, everyone; whatever happens, I hear about it.

They were all talking about him. And now they'll be talking about him even more. I'm telling you, he was a real bastard.

So that's how this holiday village turned into a cursed place.

Even so, it's the woman they pointed their fingers at. Saying she was evil, a she-devil, a monster, a killer.

So what if they killed the doctor. And others too.

Let's say she killed him with her own hands.

Did she do it just like that? For no reason? Why would she kill a doctor from a holiday village? Why would she risk her own life? She could end up rotting in prison for that.

It must mean that he did terrible things to her daughter. So she lost her head. Snapped.

Her eyes must have turned in their sockets. And she did what she had to do. How do I put it? It's like the doctor tried to steal her daughter. To steal something from that girl. And as it was, she was ill. And he was supposed to make her better.

None of us know what really happened.

Including me.

But I loved her. All kinds of people come and go, and she was like no one else.

It's just as well.

She had this way of looking at things. This way of putting things. Certain expressions. After a while I found myself using them too.

She'd look at things, things everyone else looks at, but she'd see something different. Something no one else notices.

And she'd tell you what she saw.

She was always telling her daughter. They talked all the time. They were always laughing together. They were kind of cut off, separate, like they were sitting in a box together, closed off, watching what was going on outside from inside, really seeing what was going on.

That was them.

And I tried to force myself into that box with them. For a word or two, to hear what they were saying. To see what they were seeing.

I wanted to be her son.

She could have put me in that box, no problem. And I'd have seen what she saw. Heard what she heard.

So what if they killed the doctor.

He was a bastard. He'd done terrible things. I'm sure of it. And he tried to do terrible things to that girl.

Why else would she have killed a holiday-village doctor?

They could have picked up and gone. Why get mixed up in murder? But she was so upset, she saw red. And that was that.

I loved her, and I'll never forget her.

THAT SINKING FEELING

MOTHER HASN'T BATHED for days now.

She's willing the darkness inside to show outside.

"If I bathe, if I comb my hair and brush my teeth, I'll feel as though I've done something good for myself. I might feel good about myself accidentally. But actually, I feel terrible, and that's the way it should be, Bambi. I'm in the claws of certain defeat. I've ruined everything. I'm the reason we've run out of money. I was careless. We could still be swimming in money. I was too quick to sell everything, all your grandmother's lands and possessions."

Each day is darker and more terrible. Worse than the Heavy-Heart Days, worse than Those Moments.

Before, Mother was fighting her slide into depression and desperation. She couldn't help it.

Now, Mother is punishing herself on purpose. She thinks it's what she deserves: terrible punishment. She weighs herself down inside, to hit bottom faster, fighting for air. She tells me at length. She explains in detail.

I'm terrified by Mother's attachment to the Hitting-Bottom Feeling. It's her determination to punish herself that scares me.

I don't know what to do.

"If I hit bottom, Bambi, if I force myself down to the lowest depths, like a diver driven deeper, then, when I do surface, I'll be certain to find an escape from this mess. If I do make it back up. And don't get the bends. You could say diving's risky like that."

For Mother, it's a calculated risk.

Mother's making plans for her innermost self, and she's telling me about it, all the details. And that's what I can't bear.

It's closing in on me. I can't breathe. I feel like I'll never surface.

Mother, you didn't used to make plans during Those Moments. You never considered what needed doing. You got darker and darker, closing in on yourself. You couldn't help it.

But now you're trying to achieve something; your sorrow is real, but you're doing an impression of real pain.

What's happened to you, Mother? Where have you gone? You were always disgusted by calculations, remember? What makes you do this, is it me? Because I've grown up?

"Giving birth to you gave me such a sense of achievement. I expected it to last forever. I thought the joyous thrill of getting you away from them would be enough for us, forever. Love and joy made me reckless. I thought our money would never end. All my calculations were wrong. Rather, I was unable to make any; I was unable to make sensible decisions amidst all that extravagance."

For Mother, my existence isn't enough anymore. The joy of successfully getting away each time, of running away with me, hasn't lasted, isn't enough for her now. She'd never considered how difficult it would be when the money ran out. Now she hopes for salvation in her calculation of sorrow. She hopes to rewind, regaining all we lost, just like that. She wants to believe that by punishing herself she'll be able to make it.

She almost never leaves the room.

She doesn't touch the food I bring, as though I've brought her poison. She drinks lots of water and takes handfuls of vitamins.

"You're taking your vitamins too, aren't you? And swimming for at least two hours a day? Bambi, you aren't neglecting the things you need to do, are you?"

I'm not neglecting anything. Even as you, Mother, force yourself to face your punishment and you neglect me, I'm doing my duty.

I walk along the beach, constantly. I swim three or four hours a day.

My arms have grown so long, so muscular and strong. And my legs too.

As I look at them, I can't believe they're mine. Do those long, muscular legs really belong to me? Did I do that?

I go out running in the morning, before anyone is up. How is it that during all those long walks I never thought to run?

Running is different from swimming. As I run along the beach, I'm filled with bubbles of happiness. Masses of bubbles.

I know that when I return to the room, Mother will prick them one by one. That all my happiness will leak away, the bubbles popped one by one.

I'm afraid to return to you, Mother. Your calculated despair disturbs me. Break free; come back to our world.

When I return that evening, Mother greets me with an odd light in her eye. That Sinking Feeling would never allow such a light, any light.

"I haven't even taught you how to recognize plainclothes policemen. I haven't taught you how to destroy someone, anywhere, in any room, with the first object you get your hands on."

"I know all about that."

"Plainclothes policemen are more noticeable than the uniformed ones. You can spot them a mile away—"

"I know, Mother."

I haven't taught you, because I thought there would never be any need. But I should have. I need to teach you all the things I know, one by one, everything I've had to learn."

"But Mother, you never wanted us to talk about this. You don't want this."

"Undercover policemen have sharper corners. Are better groomed. They look ridiculous as they struggle to be casual. The expressions on their faces shout it out: 'Police! Police! I'm a policeman!' And the way they look at you. It's a very human look; they know they've been caught out. It's a cowardly look. On trigger alert."

"Is it because I'm growing up? Are you telling me all this because I'm growing up, Mother, is that it?"

"I just don't know, Bambi. Never before have I had such difficulty coping with life. This isn't like the other times, when everything was out of my control. I don't want to cope anymore. I've truly hit rock bottom. And that seems perfectly reasonable, not particularly upsetting. You're right; it may be because you've grown up. You'll carry on, doing what we do. Able to run away from them on your own."

"But you haven't even told me who we're running away from."

"Bambi, come over here."

I stand directly in front of Mother. I'm taller than her, by at least four inches.

"It would be better if you weren't so tall. They'll recognize you more quickly and remember you more easily. As if your beauty weren't enough. You're easy to spot, even in a big crowd. You stand out, my beautiful Bambi."

Mother is touching my hair. She doesn't braid it anymore. She doesn't comb it, again and again. She doesn't make a ponytail, pigtails, a bun, twin buns. She doesn't bother to do anything with my hair. Or with me.

"Perhaps we'll dye your hair one day. A less conspicuous color: brown."

"But you love the color of my hair. Is it…don't you like me anymore, Mother?" I throw myself onto the bed. I'm ashamed of acting like a baby. But I've completely oriented myself to Mother. I can't bear her steady withdrawal from the corners of my soul.

Mother is abandoning me. She's forcing herself to turn into someone different. By force. I know it.

"I have to give you space, Bambi. First I have to find you a lot of money, and then I have to give you all the space you need."

"No! No!"

Mother leans forward, cups my face in her hands. "I don't regret a thing. You're the most beautiful thing I've ever done. The only beautiful thing. I lived for you, and I'm glad I did, baby."

Mother's free of That Sinking Feeling. I should have known from the light in her eye. She's risen from rock bottom. And she's surfaced knowing something. But she won't tell me. You don't need to tell me what you've learned, Mother. We're a unit. The Moon Unit. When one of us learns something, the other knows.

That's what it means to be the Moon Unit. I understand everything, Mother.

BLOODRED LIPSTICK

I SUDDENLY WAKE up.

I was having a terrible dream.

Mommy, I just had a terrible dream. I couldn't bear it. So I woke up.

I want to snuggle closer to Mother. I want to hold her without waking her. I want the smell of her to chase away the terror of my dream. You'll save me from the grip of that dream, Mother. You'll do me good, right away.

She's not here!

Mother's not in bed. I sit up and call out. "Mom! Mother!"

She's gone. Where could she be so late at night?

In my dream, something was inside my leg, a boil or pustule of some kind. I reached down, touching it with my hand. It wasn't a boil; it was a spider, and I flicked it off my leg. But there are more of them. Other spiders. There are lots of them, on my legs and my belly. As I remove one, I spot another. And another. And another. My body is covered with spider boils. Rising higher and higher. Toward my throat. And as the boils increase in number—the spiders, that is—I see how useless it is.

No matter how many spiders I get rid of, they're replaced by others. They're covering me, all of me. I'm soaked with sweat. But where's Mother? Mother, where are you?

I'm scared to go out into the corridor to look for her.

I'm scared of this hotel. Of this town.

The town has a long jetty that Mother and I walked along together. We went down onto the boulders and watched the waves. It rained all the time. It's a rainy town.

I wanted to leave immediately.

Please, Mommy, let's get out of here.

"It's cheap here," Mother says. "Let's stay a little longer."

Mother's been using that word lately, cheap. I know how much she hates it. As much as the word expensive.

I know how bad it makes her feel to use these words, as though she's sunk to rock bottom.

"It's the sense of utter failure," Mother says. "Of utter guilt, Bambi. I've failed to manage our money."

Mother's feeling lost because our money's running out. Because she has to use these words.

Staying in this town is cheap. And we'll try to stay as long as possible. Cheap. Long. A cheap town.

And the rain never stops.

We always used to leave when the rain started. We'd escape to places with no rain.

Other than walking up and down the jetty of this awful town, there's nothing to do. I hate that jetty, and the boulders on which we sit, and the dark, churning sea. I'm scared.

It scares me that we can't run away from this place, that we have to stay longer; and it upsets me, Mother, I'm telling you. And you're already sad because you have to use the word cheap.

"Like they're squeezing my throat," she says. "I'm choking. And I'm going under."

I suddenly wake up because of the spider boils. And you're not next to me. Not in our bed and not in our room. How could you leave me alone in this hotel room? How could you go off and leave me? I'm angry, worried. Are you all right? Where are you?

I gather the courage to get out of bed. I'll go to the bathroom and switch on the light. At least be in the bathroom, Mother. I'm even scared of getting out of bed and getting cold. Be there. Be there hiding to surprise me.

But Mother isn't in the bathroom. She's not on the balcony. She's not here.

I force myself to open the door onto the corridor. Our room is in a corner, at the end of a long corridor. I take a quick look. Then I slam the door shut. I'm scared to look into the corridor. Something's moving at the end of it. It seemed someone was there.

I lock the door. Then I unlock it. Mother won't be able to get in later. She'll come soon. You'll come right back, won't you, Mother?

You never go off and leave me. Where are you? Where have you gone?

I go back into the bathroom. Red lipstick rests on the shelf in front of the mirror. So red. Even redder than the plastic outside. Bloodred. It's lipstick the color Mother hates most.

Without knowing exactly what I'm doing, I put it on my lips. I give my hair fifty strokes of the brush. Counting calms me. I brush my hair fifty times. Then I lean over and let my hair hang down. Then I raise my head. My hair looks a lot fuller now, puffy.

With my puffy hair and red lips, I look like someone else in the mirror. I smile at that person. And she smiles back.

Then I'm scared of that girl with the long, puffy hair. Of her bloodred lips. I wipe it off with the back of my hand and run back to bed.

But I don't turn off the light. The minute I turn off the light, spider boils will swarm across my body.

It's silly, of course. But I can't help it. I'm scared. Mother, I'm terrified. You never leave me alone in hotel rooms. There's nowhere for you to go in this rainy town. Where could you be at this time of night?

With the last drop of my courage, I open the door again. My feet are bare. I didn't put on my slippers. I walk a few steps down the corridor and look around. Mother could be out here. Smoking a cigarette.

"Mom! Mom!"

A woman laughs at the end of the corridor. A woman's laughter. Is that a man's voice?

"Shhh!"

"Is that you?"

Something's moving at the end of the corridor. I see shadows; I hear voices.

I could walk to the end and look. Who are they?

But I'm too scared. The woman laughs again. Her voice bounces off the walls, up the corridor, reaching me.

Terrified, I close the door and lock it. My heart's in my mouth. Beating hard.

I hear footsteps. They're coming closer and closer to the room.

Now they're whispering in front of the door. The woman's trying not to laugh. Or that's how it seems to me. I'm too scared to know. She's stifling that terrible laugh, whispering with the man. What are they saying? Did they see me? Did they hear me?

A box of sleeping pills rests next to a jug of water on Mother's nightstand. She changes brands sometimes. I know Mother can't sleep without pills, that she sleeps very little.

I quickly shake three tablets into my palm. I'll swallow them and sleep. I can't bear to be this scared.

To know that they're out there in the corridor. I can't bear knowing they're there and not knowing who they are. I'm huddled in bed in fear.

Say a prayer, I tell myself. Go on, say a prayer, Bambi. I say it to myself in Mother's voice. As though she were here. Right here next to me, trying to calm me down.

Our Book of Prayer is *Bambi*, Mommy. I recite it to myself, by heart.

Bambi was often alone now. But he was not so troubled about it as he had been the first time. His mother would disappear, and no matter how much he called her she wouldn't come back. Later she would appear unexpectedly and stay with him as before.

One night he was roaming around quite forlorn again. He could not even find Gobo and Faline. The sky had become pale gray and it began to darken so that the treetops seemed like a vault over the bushy undergrowth. There was a swishing in the bushes, a loud rustling came through the leaves, and Bambi's mother dashed out. Someone else raced close behind her. Bambi did not know whether it was Aunt Ena or his father or someone else. But he recognized his mother at once. Though she rushed past him so quickly, he had recognized her voice. She screamed, and it seemed to Bambi as if it were in play, though he thought it sounded a little frightened too.

THE SEA BED

THE SEA'S SO clear here, and so lovely.

Mother and I swim all day long. We bought a huge Sea Bed at the hotel shop. A two-person Sea Bed. It's transparent. We drift out to sea on it, always.

Mother dangles an arm over one side; I dangle an arm over the other.

In soothing turquoise waters, we paddle lightly, propelling our Sea Bed. Drifting along the sea for hours.

"Our Sea Bed listens to us," Mother says. "It takes us out to the open water and brings us back to shore, obedient as can be. And it's clear and open; what you see is what you get. Nothing in the sea is hidden from us."

She smiles as she praises our Sea Bed. And I giggle. The top of the Sea Bed is shaped like a pillow. Sometimes we rest our heads there, squeezing our eyes shut. Pressing our palms against our eyelids.

Red spots begin flying before our eyes. Red butterflies and black butterflies. And if we keep our eyes shut tight, the butterflies increase in number. Butterfly Invasion, Mother calls it.

"They're swooping down on us, Bambi. Colorful butterflies covering us."

Then we open our eyes all of a sudden. As we lie there, our heads spin and spin.

We lean over and look at the bottom. Turquoise waters deepen into ultramarine.

And much later, "Picture us on the Sea Bed," Mother says to me. "Let yourself go, on the Sea Bed. Imagine rocking. Being rocked by turquoise waters. Just like I rocked you when you were a baby. Never allow anything to take this away, this stillness, this joyful buoyancy."

Mother's so happy on the Sea Bed.

As happy as when she was nursing me, she says.

"I held you in my arms for eighteen months. We stayed in one room, the two of us. And as you nursed, you were so happy, baby. Even now, I search your face for that same happiness. And as you glued yourself to my breast, your eyes and brows rolled from the sheer pleasure of it. Like a little junkie. Addiction must be something like that. Losing yourself in that optimum dose."

Mother wanted to nurse me for even longer. For two years. She wanted it to last for three years, even.

"Finally I couldn't bear it. It was the intensity of your joy, perhaps. I wasn't used to it, and I decided I had to wean you, either immediately or never. I cried as much as you did when it ended."

At great length, Mother tells me how I would stick out my tiny tongue, rejecting pacifiers, bottles, and spoons. How I wouldn't accept anything but her milk. She couldn't fool me.

"You refused to suck a pacifier, for even one day, Bambi. I couldn't get you to drink a single spoonful of water. For one-and-a-half years, it was mother's milk, and mother's milk only. That's why you're so clever and beautiful. My baby."

My grandmother never nursed my mother. In order not to deform her breasts, not to get bored. Because of her social life. So she wouldn't have to neglect her husband.

"She had so many reasons, the ice queen. And her breasts dried up, of course. That's what happens when you don't want to nurse. She couldn't admit to not being enough of a mother. She couldn't say she didn't love me or didn't want me. She could have been honest, at least. I'd have been able to love her, somewhat. I'd have been able to accept her as my mother."

"What about Father? What was he like?"

"Let's not talk about him," Mother says. "He was a snake. Even worse, unlike Mother, his venom wasn't exclusively reserved for me and our household. He was a great and important snake! He poisoned thousands, in an official capacity. And he always had plenty of poison to go around."

Mother's able to talk about them only when she's feeling well. She's so happy on the Sea Bed that she can talk about my grandparents without falling to pieces. Without going under.

"It's best to disregard them completely. Not just now. As though they never existed. That way they can't touch us. They can't reach the slopes of our souls."

"Who are we running away from, Mother? Is Father after us? Who is my father? Is he blond, like me? Do I look like him? What does he do, where does he live? Is he Turkish?"

"Bambi! Baby." Mother pulls me up onto her lap. She pulls my head to her breast.

"That's exactly what you'd do when I nursed you: fix those enormous ocean-blue eyes onto mine. When I look at you now, or while you're lying in bed, you're still my baby. Like the moment they placed you in my arms, my eyes fill with tears, even now. I'm so grateful to you for the joy you brought into my life." Mother kisses my hands. Quick, tiny kisses.

"But you're running away because of me, Mother; if I hadn't—"

"Shhh." Mother holds her long, slender fingers up to her lips. "That's not it at all. I wouldn't be alive right now. I wouldn't have been able to endure their world. I'm living for you, Bambi. And I'm happy, so full of joy, believe me."

"I'm happy too, Mom. I don't know other children, but somehow I do know. I'm the happiest girl alive. I love you so much. More than anyone could ever love."

We're bursting with happiness on the Sea Bed.

And nothing bad has happened for days. These days, the Fake Souls aren't inclined to hurt us. No one bedevils Mother with their rudeness. She hasn't been forced to protect us. It's wonderful!

We're so complete on our Sea Bed, and so happy. As we rock and drift, drowsy.

I dive into the sea to get a shell I see on the bottom. It's deeper than I expected. Shell in hand, I ascend to our Sea Bed, gasping for air.

"Look, Mom, it's huge and all pearly inside."

"You're just like my little white dog, panting and panting. When he had to pee or was bored or just wanted to go outside, he'd come up, sit at my side and pant, just like you, breathless and noisy. Take me out, I can't stand it anymore, he seemed to be saying. He had a lot of ways of talking to me, and I was the only one who understood."

"You mean the dog whose throat was cut with a piece of glass?"

"His throat wasn't cut. He grew old and fat, then he died. Who could be evil enough to cut a little white dog's throat with a piece of glass? It's not possible."

"But he's buried under the hornbeam tree, remember? We went to the Vacant Lot, in Istanbul."

"I wrapped him up in my baby blanket. Then Father's chauffeur and I took him to the Vacant Lot, and we buried him under the hornbeam tree. Did I show you the spot?"

"You showed me, Mother. You made a big gravestone for him, remember?"

"There's no one in the world sick and evil enough to cut a little white dog's throat with a piece of glass. That much we have to hope. Hold on to that hope, always. Hope that the world has never been such a terrible, unlivable place, that it never will be. OK, Bambi?"

"OK, Mother." Didn't she say they made it look like an accident? Didn't they cut her dog's throat on purpose? Was I too young to understand? Did Mother let it slip, and is she afraid now, afraid to upset me and put me off the world?

Or was she talking about a dream made real? Confusing nightmares and reality? Is it because sometimes she can't tell the difference between her dream and what's really happening?

"Come on, let's make an invasion of butterflies."

We lie on our backs on the Sea Bed. We close our eyes tight. The butterflies swoop down. Black. Red. Flitting, flying.

I won't ask for the truth.

This world upsets Mother enough as it is.

I'll never upset you, Mother. You stayed here for me. And I won't let them upset you.

MISTER MANAGER

THEN MOTHER REMEMBERED. There's land somewhere on the seaside, many acres. The last of my grandmother's properties. Land Mother hasn't sold. She put it off because she never had the energy.

We'll need to go down to that place in the South and work hard to sell the land. On top of everything else, it's in a crowded place.

"It's always full, Bambi. A place people go to be on top of one another, near the seaside."

Mother's disgusted by the delight Turks take in their own multitudes. I know how it nauseates her.

"But I think the season for them is over. They arrive together, and leave together. Like a flock of birds."

As difficult as it is for us, we go there. Even if deep down Mother doesn't want to. Mother should never be forced, should never do what she doesn't want to. When she forces herself, it all backfires and things end badly. They end for the worse.

But we've reached the end of our money. That's what Mother says. "We've hit bottom, Bambi. We have no choice. We'll have to go to that awful place to sell the land. And it must be much more valuable now. Enough money for us to live on for many years, like a basket lowered from the sky. A basket belonging to your grandmother, of course." She forces a smile. She gently strokes my hair.

Mother's so terrified of upsetting me; nothing else terrifies her. She's pretending that it will be easy to go there, to sell the land, to oversee procedures.

We go there at once. We immediately find a local broker. Mother tells him we must sell at once.

"I don't care if you sell it below or above market price," she says. "We need to leave here within forty-eight hours."

"So you're her daughter, then?" says the Broker as he looks through the deeds.

"Don't concern yourself with any of that. Just sell it, at once."

A few hours after we return to the hotel, the Broker calls. He says he has power of attorney for a wealthy client who wishes to purchase the land at once. "And at a good price, madam," he says. "You're lucky. It's just what he was looking for, a nice piece of land on which to build a few villas for his family."

"He can do what he wants," Mother says. "Whatever he wants. I'd like the money tomorrow, the moment the transaction is complete; that's all that matters."

The next morning Mother, the Broker, and I go to the registry office. The Broker is busy. Paying taxes, depositing fees.

Mother and I wait at a seaside tea garden. Then we return to the office to sign paperwork. Then back to the tea garden. The Broker is busy. He telephones from the bank. The money's arrived. He's expecting us.

"It's a lot of money," Mother says. "We're free of poverty, Bambi. We need money to escape. We need a lot of money to hide."

Mother is so happy. "Only one or two steps remain. The moment we transfer the title deed and withdraw our money from the bank, we're off to the airport. We have to hang on for just another hour or two, baby. See, saved in the forest again, by your mother."

You saved us again, Mother. Those hunters and wild animals will never be able to catch us now. You're not like Bambi's mother, confused and distracted. You never neglect me. You always manage to save us.

When we return to the registry office, we're summoned to Mister Manager's room. Mother's face turns to ash. Mother can't bear officials. She's so annoyed, I see her legs trembling.

"We seem to have a problem, madam," Mister Manager says as he flips through the documents on his desk. "We'll have to resolve it with a court ruling."

"What sort of problem?" Mother asks, struggling to control her voice.

Mister Manager peers at Mother over his spectacles. He doesn't think much of her voice or her appearance. If she were someone else, any other woman, he wouldn't be doing this. That much I know. I know that much now.

"One of the two *y*'s in your mother's given name is missing in the old deed. How am I to know if you're really her daughter? You may be someone else. The full, correct spelling of names is required in these kinds of procedures."

"You can see my date of birth, my name, my father's name. If I were someone else, would absolutely everything match up?

Is that conceivable? Why are you creating problems for me over something as ridiculous as the omission of a single silly *y*?"

"I'll be the judge of what is or isn't ridiculous! I haven't been promoted to manager for no reason." He's determined to make trouble. To destroy Mother! He has a long mustache, which he's twisting, in victory, in self-congratulation.

"You will address me with the formal 'you.' It's *siz*, not the familiar *sen*!" Mother says.

I see how difficult this is for you.

I see it in your shoulders. Why are they doing this to you?

"You're abusing your authority. Bureaucratic details and obstruction may well give you a momentary sense of satisfaction. But I simply must have these transactions completed at once. Please, I'm asking for your good services. Please help us."

"Who are you to tell me if it's *siz* or *sen*! I know who I'm addressing. File suit, have the deed changed; the burden of proof is on you. Those are the rules."

Mister Manager is red faced with rage. He removes his glasses and wipes them with a piece of cloth.

"But, sir," the Broker chimes in, "we've always sorted this kind of thing out."

My eyes are on Mother's knocking knees; she's falling to pieces, I feel it. We need to sell the land; we need the money, to escape, to survive. Why's he doing this to us? Why's he punishing us? Who are these people, Mother? Why do these Fake Souls always find us?

Mister Manager breathes on his glasses. He's far too concerned with the cleanliness of his lenses to respond to the Broker. He's enjoying himself; he's dragging it out for as long as possible. He wants only to grind us down.

"Look at me, you creature!" hisses Mother. The fountain pen in the black-marble penholder on the table is in her hand.

I don't know how it happened. It all happened in the blink of an eye.

There's a second pen in my hand.

There are two pens, one in each of Mister Manager's eyes. And the ugliest screams I've ever heard, coming from deep inside Mister Manager.

"Quick, Bambi," Mother says.

As Mister Manager's room fills with people, Mother and I take the stairs two and three at a time, until we reach the door.

"The airport!" we cry in unison as we jump into the first taxi.

"Mother, we couldn't sell the land. What are we going to do now?"

"We'll find money somehow, Bambi. But now you've—" Mother turns to face the window. She doesn't want me to see her crying.

"Mister Manager was bad, Mother. Why'd he do it to us? They are many, and bad. And we're alone."

"I never wanted this, baby," says Mother, her eyes on mine. "I never wanted you to learn just how bad the world is and to do battle against evil—"

She pulls a package of wet wipes out of her bag. "Clean your hands. And never dirty them again. Mine are dirty enough for both of us."

"But I'm a grown-up now! I won't leave you alone. Why should you face them alone?"

"You've grown up, Bambi." Mother's scratchy voice is barely audible.

"It's all for the best, Mother. The two of us, us against them."

It takes the entire package to clean our hands. "I'm tired, Bambi." Mother rests her head on my lap. She curls up.

Head on my lap, she's sleeping. Just as I've always done; she's sleeping.

Tears lick my cheeks. I lift my hand and gently catch them. These are tears of joy, Mother. Sleep well.

A   DISTANT   RELATIVE

AT FIRST I didn't recognize her.

Not that she wasn't familiar; more that I hoped it wasn't her.

I thought she was dead. We all did. We thought that the earth had opened and swallowed her up.

She couldn't be bothered to attend her dear mother's funeral, imagine that! The courtyard of the mosque was filled with mourners, so crowded that if you dropped a pin, it wouldn't hit the ground. Don't misunderstand me; I'm referring not just to any crowd, but to the finest gathering as has ever been seen in that courtyard, all there to pay their last respects.

Her husband was barely able to stand, the poor man. A distinguished gentleman, leaning on his chauffeur for support in this, his darkest hour. And as for the daughter, their one and only child, she was nowhere to be seen. It was simply inexcusable.

It's obvious to me. There's no doubt in my mind. She was responsible for her mother's death.

First we heard she was with child; the family withdrew. Then we learned of certain outrageous developments. Their family was extremely private, and naturally they shrank from the public eye. We only know what leaked out, from servants, butlers, and chauffeurs.

Her mother was a real lady, in the truest sense of the word. Reserved, uncomplaining, dignified at all times, she was the embodiment of feminine virtue.

But try as they might to keep things secret, word got out. And then: death and disaster! Just think, a vigorous woman, with no obvious health problems.

Her daughter was never seen again. Not when they withdrew into their family mansion. Not at the funeral, not when her father was taken to the hospital.

It was assumed that she'd gone abroad. That she had run off and was in hiding.

Naturally, the real truth will never emerge. All families have their secrets.

But her mother was the epitome of gracious refinement, her father a gentleman in every sense of the word. That much, I can assure you.

Her father was a most distinguished man. Absolutely devoted to his country—a man of ideas, ideas shared with his community and expounded upon in articles he penned. But he was also a man of action. I'm certain the much-lauded achievements of his great office have reached your ears as well.

I'd hoped never again to encounter her in this world.

Had she changed? She had and she hadn't. It's all in the eyes, you know.

No matter how low you're brought, what you've endured, the extent to which you've aged—the eyes, the eyes remain the same, the eyes give you away. As they say, the eyes are the windows of the soul; don't you agree?

I'd gone to that splendid hotel with two dear lady friends. Had I known what awaited me, would I have dared to do so? I can only answer in the negative.

It's the defining aspect of my character: I avoid the sight, sound, or expression of the slightest hint of unpleasantness or impropriety. Had I known I would encounter her there, I would have moved heaven and earth to avoid it. At issue here is suspicion of matricide!

No more than suspicions, they said; nothing's been proven. Be that as it may, it was all perfectly obvious to me. And later events vindicated my opinion. Otherwise, why live the life of a fugitive all these years? Why hide yourself away from human sight? It was obvious. It *is* obvious.

I noticed her little girl first.

To be perfectly frank, her very presence was deeply disturbing. In life, everything is best in moderation.

But the girl was—words fail me here—the girl was so very attractive that it was unnerving. I watched her from a distance with my lady friends—we couldn't take our eyes off her; no one could—she was frolicking in the sea all day long. Like a fish. Every time we looked, the child was there, as well as the mother.

The beauty of that child was worrying, as worrying as any kind of excess. To tell you the truth, it was disturbing.

We observed the mother as well. Dark, ungainly, unkempt. Not the slightest effort at feminine refinement. Naturally, we discussed it amongst ourselves: how could a sallow, black-maned creature like that have produced a child of such exquisite beauty, pink and white, with eyes of blue and hair spun of gold?

It would be many days before we saw her up close. Until then I watched from afar, suspicion gnawing at my heart. Had I been able to get a good look at the mother's eyes, all would have been revealed much earlier, of course.

My companions were enchanted by the child. Beauty, breed-ing, charm—and such a little lady. I swear to you they used that very word: lady.

We noticed with increasing surprise that the woman never attempted to approach us. My companions speculated over the nature of her relationship to the child. Was she the girl's mother? Who were they? Where were they from? Reclining near the beach, I listened, but made no attempt to intervene. As is my wont.

I refrained from voicing my concerns about the girl, perhaps to avoid unpleasantness and the likely rebukes of my compan-ions. I do tend to avoid disagreement at all costs.

As chance would have it, the very next day the woman and child were playing with a beach ball. The little girl would toss the ball to the woman, who would toss it back. To my mind, a tedious exercise, but still, she played the entire day, and solely to amuse the child, of course. One must give her her due. Whatever one may think about her now.

I was just about to enter the sea. The ball stopped right in front of me. I had no choice but to pick it up.

That's when the mother ran toward me.

And I handed her the ball.

As she said, "Sorry to trouble you," it struck me.

Those eyes! The unchanging mirror of the soul. Unaltered by the years. The eyes never change.

"Can it be you?" I gasped. What else could I have said?

She recognized me, I'm certain.

We're family, however distant. And I had visited them many times. Her sainted mother and distinguished father had always received me with the greatest kindness and affection.

She grabbed the ball and was gone. The little girl following her, with the most plaintive cries of "Mommy, Mommy!"

As far as I could tell, she spoke not a word to the child, who had obviously been trained to trail after her, like a stray pup.

I stood there, dumbstruck.

Her father had been such a handsome man. Deep black hair, the greenest eyes, teeth like pearls; a wonderful specimen of manhood. How I respected him, how I would hang on his every word.

The memory of that exceptional man brought tears to my eyes. I clasped my hand to my mouth and bit my knuckle to the bone to stifle the words welling within: "Murderess! I know who you are. Murderess!"

Blood ran from that knuckle, so determined had I been to keep from crying the terrible truth out loud.

But I failed to suppress my desire to see the day when all of us, the entire community, shouted that damning word after her: murderess!

If that's what they call "cursing" someone—that has never been my way but—that's what I must have done. I cursed her and her daughter both. Perhaps carried away by her despicable behavior in connection with her father's painful loss.

I lost control for a moment. And that has never been my way, I can assure you.

THE BEACH BUCKET

WE'RE ON A beach, but I don't know in which country. I'm still little. Little enough to climb onto Mother's knee and sob and sob.

Mother will always remember what happened on that beach. "Never forget your beach bucket, Bambi," she'd say, much later. "How they brought you to tears over a small beach bucket. I've never forgotten it. Your tears scorch my breast, even now."

It's a short stretch of coastline. There aren't many people. The coastline is narrow and short, or that's the way I remember it. They poured concrete over the pebbles and built outdoor showers. That's where everyone entered the sea.

There is also a tiny beach with fine sand and rowboats. That's where the ducks enter the sea. In and out. Calmly paddling along.

I watch the ducks all day long. I point them out to Mother. I'm still quite little. The same things I do all day long. And Mother does them with me.

Mother puts me to bed for my afternoon nap, in our room just over the sea. She nods off with me as she reads our book aloud to me. But when I wake up, she's gone.

When I wake up, I find Mother sitting on one of the white plastic chairs on the little balcony, legs crossed, reading and smoking. I climb onto her lap. Her hair smells of Mother and cigarettes. Her voice is infused with cigarettes, and so is her scent. Cigarettes become her, but I don't like the yellow stains they leave on her fingers and teeth. Still, if Mother's voice is scratchy, it's because of cigarettes. They're in her scent, even when she's just taken a bath. "Mother Cigarette," I called her once.

"Don't, Bambi," Mother says. "Don't throw my faults in my face. I'll get upset."

She goes to the dentist to have her teeth polished. Now they're sparkling white. I don't throw Mother's faults into her face. Anyway, Mother has no faults. Mother's perfect.

I have a swimsuit we bought in London. It's covered with Minnie Mouse heads. I have another swimsuit, with blue stripes. I don't wear bikinis, so my stomach doesn't get cold. But I love my Minnie Mouse suit. I always want to wear it. All the time.

One day we find a pair of Minnie Mouse flip-flops. We get them too. "It's a set now," Mother says. "Now your flip-flops match your swimsuit, baby."

Mother's fussy like that sometimes. If we decide to make a set, we're forever looking for things to complete it, forever adding to it. But we quickly tire of that set. That is, we quickly complete the set and have to move on to a new one.

On that day on that beach, Mother sees how much I love my purple Minnie Mouse bathing suit and becomes fixated on Minnie. When we find a Minnie Mouse bucket at the town shop, she claps her hands in delight. "Look, we've got a bucket to go with your suit, Bambi."

"But it's so little. I want this one."

The bucket I want has Winnie the Pooh, Tigger, Piglet. I love all of them; I also want a bigger bucket. Big enough to stand on. Big enough to make the highest sand castle on the beach.

"But your flip-flops and your swimsuit are a team," Mother says. "We might be able to find a Minnie Mouse towel at the open market, and then you'll have a set."

"I want the big bucket."

"Don't you want your bucket to match your swimsuit? Quick, make a decision."

"OK."

I pout a little. But I like the way Mother tries to turn everything into a complete set. It's funny. OK, Mother, as you like.

After our afternoon nap, we go down to the fine sandy beach. Mother and I use molds to make shapes in the sand. Starfish, cars, ships, fish, ducks. We make one of each. And then we'll make a sand castle right in the middle of them all. And a path of pebbles leading to it. Mother and I get down to work.

Two little girls my age come up to us. One of them has a frilly pink bikini. Her toenails are painted pale pink. The other girl is wearing beach sandals, with heels and huge flowers. I can't take my eyes off them. They whisper together as they look at us. They point.

"I'm going to get a coffee in the shade. You can play with them if you like, Bambi," Mother says in my ear.

I'd like to, Mother. I want to play with those girls. They have such funny things. I'll make the castle and the path with them.

And maybe they'll let me wear the sandals with the flowers. And teach me how to turn my toenails pink.

I begin making the sand castle on my own, but I keep looking at them. Aren't they going to invite me over?

No. They continue whispering. They giggle together. I'm getting upset, but I still want to play with them. Finally I go over.

"Oh, if it isn't the bashful little princess," says the one with the pink toenails.

"I'm not a princess," I say.

They have a fit of the giggles.

"She's a stupid princess," says the one in heels. "And she doesn't get a joke."

"Can we build a castle together?" I ask, trying to stay calm. My lower lip starts quivering. I ignore it. Maybe that's how kids speak? How am I to know? I don't know any of them.

"With that dinky bucket?" says Flowery Heels. She picks up her bucket and waves it in my face. "See this? Look how big ours is. We don't play with girls with dinky buckets like yours."

"Why not?"

"Why not?" Pink Toenails mocks. "She's bashful, she's stupid, and she has a dinky bucket, and—and—and—" They're laughing at me.

I can't bear it anymore. I start to cry, mortified. I can't understand why they're treating me so badly and why they're so bad. They're breaking my heart.

"Waaa waaa waaa," bawls Pink Toenails, wiping away imaginary tears.

"Wh-wh-why are you—?" I sob.

"We told you. Your bucket's dinky. Didn't you hear us?" Flowery Heels screams at me, one hand on her hip, waving her finger at me.

Now I'm afraid of them. I run away, leaving behind my bucket and my molds.

Mother's drinking coffee at a restaurant on the concrete beach.

"What happened, Bambi?" she shrieks, springing out of her chair.

"Mommy!" I'm choking on my tears. I can't get the words out.

"Calm down, darling. Tell me what happened. What did they do to you? Who did this to you?"

"They wouldn't play with me, Mommy. Because of my bucket, my dinky bucket. They called me a princess. And stupid."

Mother sits me down on her lap. The tears won't stop. With my head on Mother's breast, I cry and cry.

"Just imagine that, children taught at that age to humiliate a little girl just because she has a small bucket," Mother said to me, years later. "I was burning up that day. I wanted so badly to teach those girls' parents a lesson. Your tears scorched my breast. You cried right over my heart. They made you cry, for nothing. Never again did I allow you to play with children like that. Never again did I allow them to break your heart, Bambi."

Mother has no tolerance for anyone who makes me cry. Only Mother can make me cry. And I can make her cry. But Mother won't tolerate anyone else who does.

"If they upset you, they'll be punished, Bambi. They deserve it. That's why your mother's here. That's why I stayed here. To make them rue the day they upset you. To punish rudeness and evil."

I know, Mother.

I know that you've been forced to punish them.

FLIGHT

"BAMBI," MOTHER SAYS in the middle of a field of poppies. "If we had a pin, I'd teach you how to make bridal dolls out of poppies. Poppy dolls. My grandmother taught me how."

"Did you have a grandmother?"

"Of course I did, and I loved her a lot. All children have grandmothers, right, Bambi?"

"I don't. Or a grandfather. Or a father. There's no one in my life." I'm sitting on the grass. My face falls. I can't help it; I feel bad all of a sudden. Mother's had everything, and all I have is her. Only her!

"I had a grandmother, but she died when I was ten. If she'd lived longer I'd have moved to her house. I'd have had a happier life. I wouldn't have been so wounded."

"But you had a grandmother! At least until you were ten, you had one. Am I never going to have anyone but you, Mother? Won't I meet my father one day?"

Mother is sitting on the ground too. She takes hold of a valerian stem. She tries to snap it. She sinks her teeth in, midway up the stalk, and starts gnawing. She's practically eating the stalk. Chewing and spitting, chewing and spitting. She's doing this in order not to answer me, I know.

"Mommy, as happy as we are together, I still—"

"When they placed you in my arms in the hospital, you were so ugly. The doctors and nurses were beside themselves. They said they'd never seen such a lovely baby. But your face was all beet red. And wrinkled. And your neck, you didn't have a neck to speak of. You were a neckless little thing. Oh no, I said to myself."

"Were you afraid I was ugly? If I'd been ugly, wouldn't you have loved me?"

"You were ugly. You were a freakish little thing. I'd never seen a newborn before. And there you were, right under my nose. Incomprehensible, and glued to my breast. It was your self-assurance that astonished me. So sure of herself, I thought to myself, amazing. My breast is her fountain. Tiny hands pressing my skin: single-minded, carefree, certain! The truth is, Bambi, I had no idea what to do. You were completely outside my experience. Tiny, ugly, and oblivious—but you knew you had every right to be exactly where you were. At my breast, which you knew was yours and yours only."

I get up and sit down next to Mother. I take her hand in mine. Mother's scratchy voice exerts its hold on me. She's telling me something. Mother's telling me things that are important to us. Perhaps that's why I don't listen; I'm hearing her voice, not her words. Her voice: lines in the air, vertical and horizontal, turning into squares. Mother's scratchy, checked voice.

"Then they took you away from me. They cleaned my nipples with a special cream. They told me to do it every time I fed you so you wouldn't get oral thrush. They showed me how to do it. And they said they'd teach me how to clean your bottom as well. Or you might get diaper rash. They gave me an ointment containing cod-liver oil to rub onto your bottom for diaper rash."

"You didn't want me, did you?" I'd thought I was listening to Mother's voice, only not hearing her words at all, not understanding a thing.

I don't know what made me say that. It's like we're in the middle of a dream for two. Both of us having the same dream. I think I'm not talking, but I am; I think I'm not listening, but I understand every word.

"No, I didn't want you. What am I going to do with her? I thought to myself. Her mouth, her bottom, her milk. She thinks my breasts are her personal fountain, that my body's hers. She'll want my soul next. She'll take me over completely. What's more, I'll have to run away with her. Escaping alone is easy. And if I don't keep her, I might not have to run away at all. They won't pursue me, might even forget all about me, I said to myself. That's what I thought as I lay there."

"That's what you were thinking, Mother?"

"Yes, those were my exact thoughts, baby. Then they took you away from me and off to the hospital nursery. With a little plastic bracelet on your wrist. With your name on it, so you wouldn't get mixed up. You see, you were something that could get mixed up. It wasn't clear who you were or what you were; you were just someone's baby. One of many."

"Did you want to leave?"

"Yes, I wanted to leave. I wanted to leave you in the hospital that night and run away. They'll find someone for you, I said to myself. What difference does it make if I raise you or if someone else does? At least I won't have to run away with you; I'll only have to run away from you. She doesn't know me. How difficult can it be? I'll forget in no time. What I said to myself is, I'll leave you in the hospital and run away tonight."

"Well, why didn't you then? You should have left me. In the nursery." My voice shakes. So do my hands. And my legs. My whole body's shaking.

"I couldn't run off. I pictured them coming to get you. Saw them getting out of a black car, out of a door opened by their chauffeur. Saw them walking through the main entrance, clicking heels and hatred. Saw the servant girl they'd brought, ordered to pick you up. How can I leave that tiny thing with them, I thought to myself. And I thought about how you belonged to me, the way you'd lunged for my breast, the little red hands on my skin, so full of trust. Completely absorbed as you fed, transported. I started to cry. I started to sob. We can run away together, I thought. I can run with her, but not from her. I can't run away from that six-pound, beet-red wrinkled little thing. She'll be transformed into something else. Something that loves me. Something that loves me more than anyone ever could. And I'll love her more than anyone I've ever loved in my whole life. She's my daughter. My baby."

Mother's weeping in silence.

I do love her more than anyone ever has or ever will. Mother had to run away with me. She didn't want to, but she had no choice. Mother did the best she could. That's all she could do: escape, and take me with her. What else could she have done?

"Get up, Mom. Let's go back to the hotel."

I squeeze her hand, bringing it up to my lips, kissing it several times.

It was unfair of me to question Mother. So I don't have a grandmother, or a grandfather, or a father. We are what we are, Mother and me, the two of us. The Moon Unit. And though there are only two of us, it doesn't mean we're worse off than those who are many.

We're enough for each other. Complete. A unit of two.

"Wait a second, Mother." I gather poppies from the field, filling my skirt with them.

When we get back to the hotel, I get pins from reception. Mother teaches me how to remove the centers of the poppies, and how to separate them into pieces. She teaches me what her grandmother taught her. We make heads out of some pieces and bodies out of others. We make many brides, all of them with red veils and jet-black hair. Poppy brides.

The phone rings. Who could be calling us? I run over and pick up the receiver.

"They just called from the police station," the Nice Girl at reception says, "and they've checked your names and birthdates. I think they want to come and see you. I just thought I'd let you know."

"Thank you."

Mother heard what she said. "Leave everything, Bambi. We'll make do with our knapsacks."

First we lock the front door from the inside. Then we pile up all the furniture we can in front of it. We leave through the balcony door and walk out into the darkness.

"If we walk to the main road, they'll see us, Bambi."

"So what are we going to do, Mother?"

"Nothing. We'll find an out-of-the-way corner of the lobby and wait there until morning. No one will see us. Believe me, it's the last place the police would think to check. We'll stay there until morning; then we'll jump into one of the taxis bringing new guests and go somewhere new. They're closing in on us, Bambi. Now do you understand why I wanted to leave you in the hospital? I'm always running. But I didn't want to run away from you. Abandoning you was something I couldn't do. If I brought you into this world, there's a reason for it; it's best to go through life together, I thought to myself. Not just for myself, but best for you as well, I thought. Was I wrong?"

"You weren't wrong, Mother. You couldn't have left me at their mercy. I'm happiest with you. I swear it, Mother."

"No swearing! There's none of that in our religion. In our unit, I mean."

"Moon Unit!" I shout.

"Shhh," says Mother. "They notice noisy girls. They notice noisy, beautiful girls from miles away. Put your head on my lap and sleep, Bambi. Tomorrow's going to be a long day. Whereas the best days are always the shortest."

ROBBERY

THIS IS SUCH an ugly place: A Place Apart.

It's crowded. It's full. People are packed onto the beach and into the streets.

It has an ugly little square. Into which narrow alleys come to an abrupt end.

The alleys are full of shops. Nothing but shops, one after another. Cramped, side by side, hemmed in.

"Streets of jewelry shops and carpet shops," Mother says. "All selling such peculiar things. Who would buy them, and why?"

Others do so many things Mother can't understand. They wear jewels, for instance. Or drive expensive cars, or dye their hair, or get married. They always go to crowded places—

"If I understood, Bambi, perhaps I wouldn't be so filled with disgust. I wouldn't loathe their lifestyles quite so much. I haven't tried to understand them. And I never will. I can't possibly accept them as they are."

We won't attract attention here, among the crowds. We need to mingle, to blend in. They're pursuing us. Hotly.

"They're in hot pursuit, baby. I can feel their breath on my neck. We'll get away again this time. We'll have to leave the country, when they're not paying attention. But not yet. They're still on our back."

We're staying at a bed-and-breakfast popular with a young crowd. It's a noisy, dirty place near the square. We're staying here because we don't have to show our IDs.

"Off the record," Mother laughs. "We're unregistered and off the record, and we'll have to stay that way for a while. We've got to take measures, Bambi."

Actually, Mother's talking to herself. She's worried, restless and tense; all the time, every moment. Of that much I'm aware, of course.

We visit shop after shop. Just to look around, without attracting attention. That's what she wants. But why do we have to browse these stupid shops? What's the point of browsing shops heaped with things Mother hates? And she also hates that word, browse, just as I do, just as I hate everything that's happening here in A Place Apart.

We almost never go down to the beach. When we're not looking over the shops, Mother sits in the courtyard and writes in her new notebook.

"I'm getting ready, Bambi. We have no choice. If we did, believe me, I wouldn't make you stay in this suffocating place."

"It's too noisy to sleep at night. We can't sleep. Mother, please, let's get out of this ugly place right away."

"We've narrowed our list down to three shops," Mother says, ignoring me. "Down to the carpet shop on the corner and two jewelry stores. If we memorize their layouts, it shouldn't be too difficult."

"Layouts? What list, Mother? What do we care about those shops? Why should we spend any time in them?"

"I never expected the day to come when we'd be so short of money. Our resources aren't infinite, Bambi. It never occurred to me."

When Mother's forced to speak of money, she's sucked into a whirlpool of shame, down to rock bottom; I know. I don't push. I read in our stifling room, freezing when I turn on the air conditioner, boiling when I don't.

Mother spends all her time in the courtyard, drawing. I don't want to hear about her "browsing" the shops. The walls are closing in on me. I'm a prisoner, counting the hours and days until we leave this ugly place. Days spent in a waiting room of sorts; waiting for what, I don't know. Nor do I wish to. And neither does Mother wish me to.

"Closing time is best," she says at breakfast one morning.

"At night, at ten thirty or eleven, when they finally close up shop."

"Are you thinking of hiding inside?" I ask. "Until morning, to browse while no one's around?"

"If the shops weren't so small, that would be an excellent idea," Mother says. She's been inspired by a childhood film. "I'll prove to myself that I can come up with the perfect plan. No one can possibly criticize the perfection of my escape plans."

We talk like this for days, not giving it a name.

"You don't have to know everything, Bambi. I'd prefer you knew nothing of the bad things we've lived through; you know that."

"I know, Mom." You've always protected me. With my buttons switched on and off; with "forget this, Bambi," you've always sheltered me. But I'm aware of everything now, and in the middle of it. I wish I had remained forever that little girl crying in the blizzard over her stinging nose and eyes. I wish.

That night, when Mother comes up to the room from the courtyard, she's buzzing with excitement. She changes her clothes. She removes her flip-flops and puts on a pair of sneakers. She ties a pink scarf over her hair. Wrapping it round and round her head.

"They'll remember the funny pink headscarf; it's all they'll talk about. Bye, Bambi."

"What do you mean, 'Bye'? I'm coming with you."

"No, you're not. You'll wait for me here and read your book."

"Mother, have you noticed that I'm taller than you now? That I understand a lot more now? Don't pretend not to remember Mister Manager. I'm the one who's supposed to forget everything, remember?"

"That's right, you are!" Mother shouts. "I won't let bad memories stick to your soul. I never wanted you to become like me, to turn into me. You're a happy girl! I'm my mother's daughter, and I had the most miserable childhood in the world. There's no comparison. We've created certain rules for our life, and you can't break them! You can't destroy us. I won't allow it! You can't break our unit into pieces!"

"All right, Mother. I'm sorry."

The shouting has destroyed Mother's voice. She starts coughing, crazily. Her body can't bear up under all the cigarettes she's smoked over so many years; it's vomiting cigarettes. She's coughing up vomit. Her entire body is shaking.

"Shall I bring you a glass of water, Mother?"

"I'm late, Bambi." Mother slams the door on her way out. I listen to her coughing along the corridor. But now she's gone. Along with her coughs.

I hate waiting for her. I could die of worry, each and every time. It always seems like our first time apart. I don't know why. At age two I felt sick when she left me. It's the same now. The sickening wait for Mother will never end.

After some time, heavy with sorrow and worry, I fall asleep. I don't hear Mother return. I wake to the sound of the shower.

"Mom! Are you OK, Mother?"

There's no answer from the bathroom. On the plastic table directly across from the bed rests a blue garbage bag. And Mother's clothing is on the floor. Bloodied. And her white-soled sneakers, they're bloody too. Has Mother been drenched in blood from head to toe? The clothes on the floor are soaked; I can't believe it.

"Mother, are you OK? Answer me, please!" I push the door open and enter. Mother's on the floor of the shower stall, doubled over, curled up like a fetus, watching the water run red over her body.

I know immediately that something terrible has happened. What did they do to you, Mother, what happened to you?

I hold her close. Now we're both on the floor of the tiny shower stall, water running over us. Mother's face is coated with dried blood. I gently rub her face with my hands. I get some soap and lather her body.

Under my hands, Mother is like a newborn. I wash her for such a long time we both get wrinkled fingers. So be it. Mother's clean now, all clean. I take off my wet T-shirt and wrap myself in a towel. I wrap Mother in a bathrobe and take her to bed. MyBabyMother, I murmur to myself with love. You're my baby now.

"The garbage bag's full of cash and jewelry, Bambi," Mother says, brokenly. "It'll last you for years. It's the first time I had to do it for money. It was always to protect us, you and me. It was horrible! Unbearable!"

"Forget it, Mom," I say. "Forget everything that happened to you. Not just tonight. Forget everything, starting with Grandmother. We start from zero. As a Moon Unit, right from the beginning."

"Erase it," Mother says. "No, Bambi. I'll remember; you forget. That's the way it's always been, and the way it's going to be. There's a price to pay for everything. And mine is never forgetting."

BOOK OF PRAYER

"TO EACH HIS own Book of Prayer," Mother says. "Our Book of Prayer is in no way inferior or less valuable than those of others, Bambi. Only fools believe that their books alone are valuable. What's important is that everyone has a book. And is able to read it honestly and well. No Book of Prayer is of more significance or superior."

"But Mother, our Book of Prayer is *Bambi*."

"So what if it is? Every time we turn to a page, we find what we're looking for, don't we?"

I nod.

"And is it not full of signs?"

"It is, Mother. *Bambi*'s our Rocket Flare. We can even look up what's going to happen to us."

"We chose it, Bambi. It was right for us. We made it our Book of Prayer. When I was a young girl, I read other Books of Prayer as well. One by one, line by line. Believe me when I tell you, I found nothing more meaningful than what's contained in the pages of *Bambi*. To each his own Book of Prayer."

"To each his own Book of Prayer," I repeat after her, as though in prayer.

"Most people think it ends with the death of Bambi's mother. In fact, Bambi's mother dies halfway through. And the fawn grows up and makes a life for himself in the forest."

"I know, Mom."

"But most are of the opinion, however preconceived, that it ends with the mother's death: possibly because they think that's how it must end."

"His mother dies in the middle. Bambi lives, grows up, marries, has children."

"Grows up, marries, has children." Mother laughs as she makes the same hand motion: with the index finger of one hand, she touches in turn the fingers of her other hand, reeling them off, one by one.

"There's nothing special about *Bambi*. It answered our needs; it was there. We made it our Book of Prayer. As others have done with their Books of Prayer. Nothing more, nothing less. We loved it, and we depended on it. But we don't mock the books of others just because our book is *Bambi*; do we, my Bambi?"

"No, we don't mock them, Mom. We don't mock their books, or anything else about them."

I'm sitting on Mother's lap under a great tree, huge white blossoms bursting forth among slippery leaves.

"Like they've opened up umbrellas," I say to Mother.

Mother kisses me on the nose. "The white umbrellas of the invisible wood sprites," she says. "If we nod off here under the tree, perhaps they'll show their beautiful faces."

"Come on, Mother, read *Bambi* to me a little," I plead. "Let's go to sleep. I wonder what we'll dream? Will the sprites come out?"

Bambi heard steps and looked behind him. He was there. He came bursting through bushes on all sides. He sprang up everywhere, struck about him, beat the bushes, drummed on the tree trunks and shouted with a fiendish voice.

"Now," said Bambi's mother. "Get away from here. And don't stay too close to me." She was off with a bound that barely skimmed the snow. Bambi rushed after her. The thunder crashed around them on all sides. It seemed as if the earth would split in half. Bambi saw nothing. He kept running. A growing desire to get away from the tumult and out of reach of that scent which seemed to strangle him, the growing impulse to flee, the longing to save himself were loosed in him at last. He ran. It seemed to him as if he saw his mother hit but he did not know if it was really she or not. He felt a film come over his eyes from the fear of the thunder crashing behind him. It had gripped him completely at last. He could think of nothing or see nothing around him. He kept running.

My head in Mother's lap, I begin to nod off. Mother pulls up an end of the blanket we're sitting on and wraps it around me. She leans her head against the tree trunk. Mother's pretending her eyes are closed. Mine flutter shut.

"Mom, Bambi never sees his mother again," I say sleepily.

"It happens in the middle of the book. Bambi's story continues, later. He experiences so many things. Come on, go to sleep, Bambi."

"Pleasant dreams, Mommy. Dreams of sprites." And I doze off, then and there.

When I wake up I find Mother sitting under a different tree, watching me.

"Couldn't you sleep, Mom?"

"I slept. But a bad dream woke me."

"Go on, tell me all about it."

"No, it was bad. You tell me yours."

"Umm, my dream had wood sprites. They opened their white umbrellas, and they were dancing. And their leader was an old sprite. And she had a bright blue umbrella. Hers was the only blue one, though. And then—"

"And then?" Mother knows I'm making up my dream as I go along. Because I can't remember what I dreamed. But if I tell her about my dream, she has to tell me hers. That's how we've always done it.

"Then the old sprite said, to all of them—well, first she shook her finger, like this—and then she said, 'Keep your umbrellas clean. Keep them clean at all times. White as snow.'" I frowningly imitate the old sprite.

Mother's laughing so hard she's rolling on the ground. "Oh my, what a disciplinarian; that strict old sprite's a regular empress! What an authoritarian, what a dictator!"

"A what, Mother?"

"I'm improvising," says Mother, tears shining in her eyes. "So, what else did she say to her wood sprites?"

"Oh, and she also said, 'Dance. Dance beautifully.' And she said, 'And swim a lot in the rivers. The more you swim, the better. You're my world-champion sprites.'"

"Hmmm… Might there be something of me in that old sprite? That bit about swimming sounds a little familiar." Mother's holding her sides, laughing. Once she starts, she can't stop, and never could.

And I laugh with her. I'm laughing. Every now and then, Mother shakes her finger at me, imitating the old wood sprite. We laugh so hard, our stomachs hurt.

"Come on, let's go back to the hotel. It's getting shivery, Bambi."

"I don't say 'shivery' anymore, Mother! I know to say 'It's getting cold'!"

"Good for you, you're Mommy's big girl." Mother gathers up all our things and kneels. I get up onto her back and she grips my hands to hold me steady. "Wood sprites! Get out of the way, wood sprites, off we go!" my unicorn cries as she carries me back to our room.

"It's your turn now."

"My turn for what, baby?"

"Your turn to tell me your dream. I told you. And if you hadn't died laughing, I'd have told you even more. There was more. It was kind of long, actually."

"I had a dream about your grandmother. It was a bad dream, Bambi. You didn't know her, you wouldn't understand even if did tell you."

"But Mother—"

"It was just a dream, like the other ones, where I'm in a room and I see your grandmother sitting in an armchair. She's looking at me; or, more accurately, she's observing me. I'm afraid."

"But why, Mother?"

"Because she's not dead. She deceived everyone. She never died. She's been hiding, to punish me. She pretended to die, but she's alive. When I see her there, I feel terrible. Because she deceived me and because I'm afraid of her."

"What happens next?"

"I talk to her. 'Aren't you ever going to forgive me, Mother?' I ask. 'Aren't you going to love me, just for one day? Aren't you going to want your daughter even as much as a mother crow?'" Mother's voice trembles. It comes and goes.

"That's terrible, Mom. What does Grandmother say then? Does she hug and kiss you?"

"She always had a certain sideways look. That's how she's looking at me, full in the face, coldly. 'You'll get your punishment!' she says."

"And what do you say, Mom?"

Mother's voice is in knots now. "'My punishment was you, Mother,' I say. And then I woke up."

THE SOLDIER

THEIR HOTEL WAS in our zone, under our jurisdiction.

I wish it hadn't been; that's what I thought to myself later. I wish the police had come.

If the police had come instead of us, none of this would have happened. Perhaps. But what do I know?

Our first lieutenant's a real creep, a real stiff-necked creep. When it comes to the gendarmerie, I mean. And he's so set on rising through the ranks. It's all he thinks about!

He's got his eye on high places. Says he's going to become a commander or a commander in chief. Goes on about it all the time.

Yeah, right! I got news for you: you're a gendarme! A rural police-soldier is all you are. But try saying that to his face. He's got a quick temper, that one. Ask around, they'll all tell you the same. They'll tell you they've never seen anyone so quick to hand out penalties, that the guy's a real nutcase. And always on our backs about something.

But what can you do? When you're ticking off the days, they go by pretty quick. Next thing you know, your military service is done and you're back home. And your days as a soldier are forgotten. At least you hope they are. I mean, I hope I don't remember a thing. Not a single minute.

And as for this last incident, well, it's kind of like it ripped open a hole in me, right here, in my chest. And I don't know if it'll ever close up. I mean, I don't know if I'll ever forget, no matter how hard I try. It's like a crater. You know, a crater like the one a tossed grenade makes. That's how I picture it.

Some guy at reception called us. I guess he had it in for that mother and daughter. OK, so they'd been in the papers, but if that guy hadn't gotten all suspicious, hadn't butted in, hadn't called the station—

You know, there are types like that in life. Take-charge types. And if my first lieutenant hadn't been the same way, hadn't seen it as the chance of a lifetime—

He'd already been fighting out in the East. He was forever blabbing on about it something awful. All the terrorists he blew away. Well done! Just keep on bragging about it, for the rest of your life. But in the end, you ended someone else's life.

I mean, I wouldn't want to kill anyone. I was relieved when they drew lots, when I found out I wasn't being sent to the East. All that boasting about the bodies he left behind, the number of guys he killed! I wouldn't feel right about something like that. And I'd never forget. I might have a kid one day and feel bad, looking at my kid. They've all got mothers and fathers, after all. I guess that's kismet for you. Here I was, posted to a nice place like this, and look what happened. I must have been fated to see what I saw. And I'll never forget it. If only I hadn't been on duty that night, if only I'd been passed out, sleeping. And hadn't seen any of it. Now there's no way I'll ever forget it.

It doesn't matter what they tell you; you're never ready for something like that. You think they're exaggerating, your mind wanders. Well, seeing is believing. It must be because she was a woman, a mother, and it happened right in front of her daughter—I don't know. The whole thing shook me up pretty bad, I can tell you that much.

They were running off into the night. Packs on their backs, running for dear life. They must have known we were coming. So they jumped off the balcony and ran for it.

He cut them off in the garden. "Halt! Gendarme!" he shouted. Showing off, all the usual crap. A megaphone, even.

But they just hightailed it right out of there. Mother and daughter. I'd have let them keep running, off into the darkness. That's what I'd have done. I wouldn't have had the stomach to do anything else.

The lieutenant didn't even bother to repeat himself. He opened fire, just like that. Like his machine gun was a finger or something. A finger he was waving back and forth, spraying bullets right and left.

What if something had happened to the girl? He could have killed her too! But it was the mother we were after. She was the guilty one. What if he'd killed that beautiful girl? His finger on the trigger, rat-tat-tat-tat.

The woman keeled over onto the grass, right in front of our eyes.

She'd taken so many bullets, all she could take, really. Her whole body pumped full of holes.

But it was the strangest thing: as she was falling, down onto the grass, it was as if she gave us one last look. It seemed she was smiling. You know, one of those fuck-you-all smiles. That was the look she had on her face.

She didn't say anything, of course. I'm just telling you what it seemed like to me. No woman would ever talk like that, of course. But the look, yeah, she was telling us to go fuck ourselves, no doubt about it. Or at least that's how I saw it. And she was definitely smiling.

But before she was sprayed with bullets, before that maniac lieutenant of ours let loose on her with his machine gun, she shouted something to her daughter. "Run!" she said. "Run, baby!" Except she didn't say baby. It sounded like baby, but it wasn't. I know she said run, I'm sure of that much.

So the girl runs off with a garbage bag in her hand and a pack on her back. Never even looked back. Just disappeared into the darkness.

We all crowded in around the mother, of course. The lieutenant ran over first.

He had to make sure she was dead. She's lying there full of bullet holes, and he's making sure she's dead.

OK, I know she was trouble. I don't even know how many people she killed. People say an eye for an eye and all that.

And again, maybe it was because she was a woman, a mother, but she didn't make a sound when she was getting pumped full of bullets. Not a sound. "Run," she said, and then something that sounded like "baby." And then, nothing.

I saw their pictures in the paper the next day. Her daughter was such a beauty. Not a trace of her now. They can't find her. And they never will.

If she was able to run away while her mother was getting shot, she's not going to pop up now and say, "Here I am," is she?

From what I read, that's how she was raised. I mean, on the run, running from hotel to hotel.

There was a bunch of stuff about them in the paper, but it was mostly about the woman's mother and father.

That's because no one really knew much about the mother or the girl. Except for the other murders.

What I want to know is, how can they be so sure? Now that's she's dead, they'll just pin everything they can on her, of course. Now that she's dead.

And as for our lieutenant, well, he was a hero for a couple of days.

No one asked him if he could have caught her alive. Even though they didn't find any weapons on her.

He could have shot her in the leg. He could have caught her that way. The courts could have punished her.

But he was used to all that heroism out in the East. So he raked her over. That's the only word for it. Raked. He mowed that woman down.

Until she was full of bullet holes.

But what'd she do? She smiled. She smiled with a look on her face that said, "Fuck you all, the whole lot of you!"

Maybe I'm out of line here. I could be putting words in her mouth; that is, in her head.

But it makes sense to me. Look at how she lived her life. A woman like that? What she did. Even while she was getting pumped full of lead.

The whole thing made me sick. Maybe I'm just trying to see the bright side. Could be.

Or it might be that in my heart of hearts I want to believe that that's how she died. To make myself feel a little better. I don't know.

If the police had come instead of us, if they'd been in charge of the area, of the hotel, it might have turned out differently. She might still be alive today. In prison.

I'm not saying she shouldn't have been punished.

It's just tough to see a woman mowed down in the night like that, right in front of you.

If the girl had come back, if she'd crouched down over her mother's body and cried and carried on—it might have been better.

For the woman. And for us.

No. Actually, it wouldn't have been. I mean, she was dead before she hit the ground. She must have been. With all those bullets?

OK, she was a criminal; we don't know how many lives she took. Fine then, she deserved to die. Let's say it all turned out for the best. Let's say that.

But the sight of my lieutenant standing there, right next to her, booting her in the head, well, that's what finished me off.

She was dead. You'd raked her with bullets, she was full of holes. So why are you kicking her in the head?

That's what I'll never forget. That scene with him booting her in the head. I can't help thinking how fucked up things are. It really is a fucked-up world we live in, no doubt about that.

There's a woman, a mother, lying there on the ground. Dead. Why kick her in the head? Why the hatred? And in whose name? And why?

ABOUT THE AUTHOR

Photograph © Tomasz Kowalski

Born in Istanbul, Perihan Magden has written novels, poetry, and a column in Turkey's national daily newspaper, *Radikal*. She is the author of four novels, three of which—*Messenger Boy Murders, 2 Girls*, and the recently released *Ali and Ramazan*—are currently available in English; *The Companion* has not yet been translated. *2 Girls* was made into a film by director Kutlug Ataman and premiered at the 2005 London Film Festival. Magden's novels have been translated into eighteen languages, including German, French, Spanish, Italian, Greek, Portuguese, and Dutch. She is an honorary member of English PEN and winner of the Grand Award for Freedom of Speech by the Turkish Publishers Association.

ABOUT THE TRANSLATOR

 Born in Salt Lake City in 1964, Kenneth Dakan is a freelance translator and voiceover artist who has translated numerous works of fiction and nonfiction from Turkish to English, including Ayşe Kulin's *Farewell: A Mansion in Occupied Istanbul* and *Sevdalinka*, Ece Temelkuran's *Deep Mountain: Across the Turkish-Armenian Divide*, Buket Uzuner's *Istanbulians*, and Mehmet Murat Somer's *The Prophet Murders*, *The Kiss Murder,* and *The Gigolo Murder.* In 2011 and 2012, Dakan participated in the Cunda Workshop for Translators of Turkish Literature.